PRAISE FOR RODRIGO REY ROSA

"Rey Rosa creates narratives of mythic proportio
San Francisco Chronicle

"Rodrigo Rey Rosa is one of the most interesting Latin American writers of his generation."
ERNESTO CALABUIG, *El Cultural*

"A colossal writer in the Spanish language who, with the prodigious exactitude of his prose and the mathematic equilibrium of his narratives, draws from an abundance of techniques amplified by true talent."
JAVIER APARICIO MAYDEU, *El Periódico*

"His work is extraordinarily precise, mythic, and intriguing; it's literature without useless gestures, where beauty seems to be born of its author's curious inclination toward silence."
RAPHAËLLE RÉROLLE, *Le Monde*

"Rodrigo Rey Rosa has developed a signature prose style with which he is cultivating one of the most impressive careers in Latin American literature. Known best for his winning short stories, his writing sometimes draws from the influence of magical realism and at other moments reaches almost Baroque sensibilities, achieving a poetic elegance that is both lucid and precise."
RICARDO BAIXERAS, *El Periódico*

"Rodrigo Rey Rosa's prose, dense and precise, shows his literary relationship to legendary writer Paul Bowles."
Der Spiegel

"Each new book by Rodrigo Rey Rosa . . . [has] the special quality of a meticulous prose, elaborate to the point of being hand-crafted though not in search of style, but rather, on the contrary, of writing that is refined, light, silent, that is evocative and imaginative rather than informative. In *Severina*, the books serve as some of the protagonists, but the novel isn't bookish because the books 'vibrate and breathe' . . . we're able to succumb to the romantic delirium and the quixotic passion for books as both objects and interpretations."
J. A. MASOLIVER RÓDENAS, *La Vanguardia*

Severina

Severina

RODRIGO REY ROSA

TRANSLATED BY CHRIS ANDREWS

YALE UNIVERSITY PRESS ■ NEW HAVEN & LONDON

A MARGELLOS
WORLD REPUBLIC OF LETTERS BOOK

The Margellos World Republic of Letters is dedicated to making literary works from around the globe available in English through translation. It brings to the English-speaking world the work of leading poets, novelists, essayists, philosophers, and playwrights from Europe, Latin America, Africa, Asia, and the Middle East to stimulate international discourse and creative exchange.

Yale University Press books may be purchased in quantity for educational, business, or promotional use. For information, please e-mail sales.press@yale.edu (U.S. office) or sales@yaleup.co.uk (U.K. office).

Set in Electra and Nobel types by Keystone Typesetting, Inc.
Printed in the United States of America.

Library of Congress Cataloging-in-Publication Data
Rey Rosa, Rodrigo, 1958–
[Severina. English]
Severina / Rodrigo Rey Rosa ; Translated by Chris Andrews.
         pages   cm — (The Margellos World Republic of Letters)
"Originally published in Spanish as Severina, copyright © 2011, Rodrigo Rey Rosa."
ISBN 978-0-300-19609-2 (alk. paper)
I. Andrews, Chris, 1962– translator. II. Title.
PQ7499.2.R38S4813   2014
863'.64—dc23   2013024355

A catalogue record for this book is available from the British Library.

This paper meets the requirements of ANSI/NISO Z39.48-1992 (Permanence of Paper).

10 9 8 7 6 5 4 3 2 1

For Beatriz Zamora

.

CONTENTS

Introduction by Chris Andrews   ix

Severina   1

Acknowledgments   87

INTRODUCTION

CHRIS ANDREWS

Readers who look to Central American literature for baroque exuberance, perhaps with the prestigious precedent of Miguel Angel Asturias in mind, are likely to be surprised by the Guatemalan Rodrigo Rey Rosa. His fiction is the opposite of lush: generally spare in style, restrained in its exploration of the characters' inner worlds, and elliptical in structure. Moreover it tends to be somber in tone. These descriptive formulas might, in North America, suggest that Rey Rosa belongs to the numerous offspring of Hemingway, but that would be a somewhat misleading impression, for he is not a writer who begins from a secure (if bleak) sense of how things really are. In the fiction of Rey Rosa the lincaments of the real cannot be taken for granted. It is true that his settings have gradually become more particular and identifiable, and that the fantastic and speculative elements that marked his first three books—*The Beggar's Knife, Dust on Her Tongue,* and *The Pelcari Project,* all translated into English by Paul Bowles—have since receded. Nevertheless, dream, fantasy, and hallucination still threaten the stability of the worlds in which his characters live. In this regard, Rey Rosa remains fruitfully in debt to the writer whose work revealed his vocation: Jorge Luis Borges.

The difficulty of distinguishing dreams from experience of the world we share is written large in *Lo que soño Sebastián* ("What Sebastian Dreamed," 1994). The title poses a question to which the novel replies in a deferred and partial manner: Did the protagonist dream that he was forced to fire a shotgun or was he effectively framed for the murder of his neighbor? Is he the victim of a nightmare induced by fish eggs gone bad or of a home invasion? Quandaries of this nature are pivotal in a number of Rey Rosa's stories and novels. Rather than blurring the action, they make it tremble like a clear reflection on rippled water.

Rey Rosa's fiction departs from a narrowly conceived realism in another way as well: it sometimes gives onto a mythical or allegorical hinterland, delicately intimated, never insisted upon. Sometimes the characters' names suggest that they stand for something beyond their particularities, as in "Gracia," a story from the collection *Otro zoo* ("Another Zoo," 2007), whose eponymous heroine prays to God that she may be taken as a sacrificial victim instead of the lamb she has been raising, which her entrepreneurial brother has sold to a Muslim neighbor for the feast of Eid ul-Kbir. "Gracia" (the noun *gracia* means *grace* but also *mercy* or *pardon*) patently alludes to Abraham's sacrifice, but is not a simple inversion of the scriptural episode, which, rather than serving as a key, gives Rey Rosa's vividly realistic fiction, set in contemporary Guatemala, an enigmatic resonance. In *The African Shore* (Yale University Press, 2013), set in Tangier, the revelation of the protagonist's name is strategically delayed until the moment he is about to lose it, along with his passport and his life, to a mysterious assailant. The name revealed—Angel Tejedor—is common enough yet, in context, irresistibly significant, for *tejedor* means weaver, and this is precisely when the drifting protagonist overcomes his passivity and, in vanquishing his Doppelgänger, recovers a minimal capacity to weave the threads of his fate.

Having lamented the range and quality of books for sale in Guatemala City, the narrator of *Severina* adds: "There are far more serious problems here, but I don't want to talk about all that now." Taking a break from those serious problems, *Severina* is an exception among the recent novels of Rodrigo Rey Rosa in that it only glances momentarily at Guatemala's pervasive politico-criminal violence, which is confronted in a particularly direct and courageous way in *El material humano* ("The Human Material," 2009). Nevertheless, the novel shares the characteristics just outlined: the instability or inscrutability of the real and a mythical or allegorical hinterland. The narrator is an eclectic reader, an aspiring but stalled writer, and part-owner of a bookstore. Into his stagnant life comes a beautiful thief: Ana Severina Bruguera Blanco. She steals from his store and manages to foil the alarm system. Although eventually receptive to his advances, she remains fundamentally elusive and inscrutable. Where, for example, does she come from? Sometimes the narrator can hear an Argentine or Uruguayan accent when she speaks, but at the *pensión* where she is staying she gives her nationality as Honduran. What is the nature of her relationship with the old gentleman, Otto Blanco, who shares her room at the Pensión Carlos? Is he her father, as she says at first? Or her husband, as the narrator's friend and fellow bookseller Ahmed al Fahsi asserts? Or her grandfather, as Señor Blanco himself explains? Is she a petty thief or a kleptomaniac? Or does her way of life reflect a radical existential choice?

These questions haunt the narrator, but very soon it is too late for the answers to make a difference in how he will act: he is deliriously in love. Increasingly the reader is led to envisage a possibility that the narrator himself cannot quite bring himself to face, perhaps because it seems outdated and unenlightened: "The incoherent images that tumbled through my mind left me thinking that the idea of love that comes down to us from the Romantics, who associated it with death and sometimes with the devil, was too gloomy to be credible, much less desirable, these days." This characterization of the romantic idea of love seems to be influenced by one of the books that Severina steals: Mario Praz's *La carne, la morte e il diavolo* (published in English as *The Romantic Agony*), which contains a chapter on the Fatal Woman titled "La Belle Dame Sans Merci."

As to the novel's mythical hinterland, it is suggested by the speech in which Otto Blanco presents himself and Ana Severina as members of a maligned tribe, the gypsies of the book trade, so to speak, exploiting its ebbs and flows "beyond literary good and evil." Toward the end of the novel Ana Severina remembers her grandfather saying that one of their remote ancestors invented dice. "A man from Lydia. It's in Herodotus. His people emigrated to the north of Italy because of a famine that lasted for many years." The reference is to *The Histories*, volume 1, section 94, in which Herodotus explains that during a "grievous dearth" (as G. S. Macaulay translates the passage) the Lydians discovered "the ways of playing with the dice and the knucklebones and the ball . . . as a resource against the famine . . . —on one of the days they would play games all the time in order that they might not feel the want of food, and on the next, they ceased from their games and had food." But since the famine persisted, half the Lydian people were sent abroad and finally settled in "the land of the Ombricans," that is, in Umbria, where Ana Severina says she spent her childhood.

Señor Blanco does not reveal exactly how his tribe has operated through the ages, but Ana Severina has a bibliophile's eye for the precious collectible (she steals a first edition of Émile Laoust's anthology of Berber tales—"a treasure"—from Ahmed al Fahsi) and a true reader's eye for the obscure or forgotten gem. "She would come back with new books—often titles I'd never heard of—and there was almost always an extraordinary discovery among them," says the narrator, who lists her spoils. It is tempting to presume that the lists encrypt a secret, and the narrator himself gives way to this temptation at one point: "I kept going over the books that she had taken from me and trying to imagine the complete list of every title she had ever stolen. It was as if I thought this would help solve the mystery of a life that seemed bizarre and fantastic to me." But there are two other ways to read the lists, which will, I think, prove more rewarding in the end. First, as multilingual collage-poems, alluding occasionally to the novel's themes: *Severina*, too, is *Une ténébreuse affaire* ("A Shadowy Affair," Balzac) and the origins of its female protagonist are mysterious, as in *La española inglesa* ("The Spanish-English Woman," Cervantes). Second, the lists can be read in a simpler and more outward-looking way as homage paid to lesser known works, worth hunting out in second-hand bookstores. As Otto Blanco says: "There are wars between different kinds or genres of books. . . . And, as in real wars, the best don't always win."

Like Severina and Otto Blanco, the narrator and Ahmed al Fahsi exploit the ebbs and flows of the book trade. Ahmed says they are "like alchemists," a reflection prompted perhaps by the book he has been reading—*Conversations Between Alchemists* ("Conversaciones entre alquimistas") by Jorge Riechmann— which he gives to the narrator as a present. Perhaps the gift is also prompted by the book, in which Riechmann writes: "Capital wants to make us believe that we are what we sell. But we are what we give away." Ahmed does seem strongly influenced by Riechmann, for the words the narrator overhears him saying on the telephone—"There's no money for the famine in Africa, but there's money to send satellites into space"—are lifted almost verbatim from *Conversations Between Alchemists*, as the narrator finds out (but indicates in a way so subtle it could easily be missed) when he opens the book at random. Here it seems that a book is exploiting its reader, using him to propagate its content, as if it were animated by an autonomous spirit, in line with the beliefs of Otto Blanco's eccentric uncle, for whom books are the agents of a global struggle for domination.

There are, however, limits to Ahmed's generosity, for he intends to make Severina pay in full for her thieving, one way or another. The narrator, on the other hand, declines Señor Blanco's offer to reimburse him for the stolen books and eventually tires of the "alchemy" of converting printed matter into gold: "I had begun to feel that there was something crass about simply trading books for money." He longs to escape from the book trade and into the gift economy of art (when he tells his friends he wants to go away and "try his luck at writing a novel," he is hiding the main reason for his decision to travel, but not necessarily lying). Similarly, toward the end of the novel, having committed himself to a large and indefinite expense for the sake of love, he feels "released from . . . an ingrained but strange vanity—the obscure vanity of the single man."

In Rey Rosa's fiction, access to the characters' mental worlds is limited. This is not to say forbidden: he is not a behaviorist writer. When we enter the minds of his characters, it is most often through fear. Fear with its physical symptoms and its complex phenomenology, fear not as a weakness or an illness but as a fact of daily life in certain societies, is a central motif in Rey Rosa's work. Here *Severina* is, again, exceptional, because we enter the narrator's inner world through desire and anxious longing. Yet fear is not altogether absent, for if love releases the narrator from the vanity of the single man, he is released into unknown territory. The object of his love remains in many ways a blank (as Severina's matronym Blanco suggests). The uncertainty surrounding her identity and her nature is artfully sustained, and Rey Rosa's skill in balancing ambiguities is evident when Severina shows Ahmed a copy of the Koran she claims to have stolen from Borges's library, on a page of which the Argentine master has apparently made a note toward one of his stories: "The Mirror of . . ." This is presumably "The Mirror of Ink" from *A Universal History of Infamy*, which contains a quotation from the Koran, and in which a tyrant's desire to know and see all precipitates his violent death. But by cutting the title short Rey Rosa also alludes to a later text by Borges, the essay "The Mirror of the Enigmas" from *Other Inquisitions*, which glosses Léon Bloy's unwittingly cabalistic variations on I Corinthians 13:12: "For now we see through a glass, darkly; but then face to face: now I know in part; but then I shall know even as also I am known." If, as Borges imagines in a footnote to that essay, we are tracing a significant figure with every step we take, the nature of that figure is not ours to see, not, at any rate, on this side of the glass or the mirror. In the last three sentences of *Severina*, the narrator, imagining the future and the unknown figure he is tracing, uses the word *perhaps* (*quizá*) three times. It is, I think, one of the key words of this brief and limpidly written novel, which, like all of Rodrigo Rey Rosa's fiction, ripples over dreamlike and unquiet depths.

Severina

What power has love but forgiveness?
—William Carlos Williams, "Asphodel, That Greeny
Flower," Book 3

I noticed her the first time she came in the store, and right from the start I picked her for a thief, although that day she didn't take anything.

On Monday afternoons there were usually poetry readings at La Entretenida, the bookstore I'd recently opened with a group of friends. We didn't have anything better to do and we were tired of paying through the nose for books chosen by and for others, as "eccentrics" like us are forced to do in provincial cities. (There are far more serious problems here, but I don't want to talk about all that now.) So, to put an end to this annoyance, we decided to start our own store.

I had just split up with the latest love of my life, a Colombian woman. It had been both simple and impossibly complicated, a waste of time or a wonderful adventure, depending on your point of view.

The bookstore wasn't very big, but at the back there was room to set up tables and chairs for the events, which varied from straightforward readings to performances and burlesque.

When I saw her come in that first afternoon, a downpour had flooded the passages in the basement of the little shopping center where we had our premises; the clients had to walk from store to store on planks supported by blocks of cement and recycled bricks. She was wearing tights with high, flat-heeled boots and a white cotton blouse. Her hair was very black. She didn't seem all that young. She left before the end of the reading (of prose poems, which sounded very good to me), but I knew she'd be back.

From one afternoon to the next I kept waiting for her. Why was I so sure that she'd be back? I wondered. I didn't know.

Eventually, one Monday afternoon, she turned up. The reading had already begun. She stood by the curtains that separated the main part of the store from the little space where the readings were held. This time she was wearing a rather loose-fitting dress made from a single piece of blue cotton, which came down to her knees (perfectly rounded knees they were, shaped with evident care), a broad silver-plated belt, and black leather sandals. She was carrying a sequined handbag. She stayed until the end. She went to get a drink at the bar, exchanged glances and greetings, and, before leaving, slipped two little books from the Japanese literature section into her bag. The speed of it was impressive. Then she walked out through the door in no hurry at all. The alarm didn't go off; I wondered how she'd done it. I let her go: again, I was sure she'd be back.

A moment later I went over to the Japanese shelf. I noted down the missing titles in a ledger, along with the date and the time. Then I went to the cubicle that enclosed the cash register and sat there, trying to imagine where she would go with the books.

The next time, two or three weeks later, when I saw her come in, I said good afternoon and asked if she was looking for something in particular.

"Yes, I'm looking for a present," were the first words I heard her say.

"Can I ask who it's for?"

"For my boyfriend," she said. She had an unidentifiable accent.

"Well, you're the best judge. There are some new books in the Japanese literature section."

Her face lit up.

"Ah," she said, "I love Japanese literature."

"It's over there." I pointed to the far side of the store. "As you know."

She didn't react. All she said was: "He's not so keen on it, though. It's too fashionable; that's what he says anyway. Do you have something by . . . Chesterton?"

I let out a hollow laugh. "OK, that sort of guy. We must have something. It'll be over there," I pointed to the opposite side of the store, "on the top shelf. Yeah, with the Cs."

I went back to the cash register and started flipping through catalogs, to put her at ease. She wandered back and forth between the shelves. I thought I heard her slipping a book into her bag (a volume of Galland's translation of *The Thousand and One Nights*, as I was to discover).

A few minutes later she came to the register and said: "No luck. I'll get him some after-shave."

"Come back whenever you like." I stood there watching her. She walked out through the security gate, and once again the alarm remained mute.

I went to the plundered shelf. In the ledger I noted: *The Thousand and One Nights*, volumes 1, 2, and 3, then added the time and the date. I decided that one day I'd follow her when she left.

A few days later we received a batch of books that included a collection of translations from Russian. They were small, sextodecimo-format volumes with engravings and gilded initials: beautifully crafted, a pleasure to read, perfect as jewels. I put them on a shelf quite close to the cash register, but made sure that some couldn't be seen by the person who was serving. Those volumes were for her.

It was on a Thursday, almost a month later, that I decided to act. We were alone in the store, just the two of us, and she was browsing under my discreet surveillance. I didn't mention the new Russian collection; I had greeted her vaguely when she came in, pretending to be absorbed in some financial documents.

She didn't hear me. I came up behind her so close I could smell the scent of her hair.

"Where have you hidden them this time?" I asked. She started, spun around, and bumped into me.

"What!" she cried. "You frightened me! What do you want? Are you crazy?" When she saw that I was smiling, she laughed.

"Sorry."

She put her hand on her chest, covering her neckline. "You really scared me."

"I really want to know where you've hidden them."

Now she was cross; a fine line appeared between her thick, dark, shapely eyebrows. She pushed me aside and started walking hurriedly toward the door. I reached out, pressed a button, and although she ran the last few steps the security grille came down just in time to block her exit. She stopped and shoved at it.

"This is outrageous," she said and turned to look at me. She took a cell phone from the pocket of her trousers and dialed a number. "Either you let me out or I'm calling for help."

"Calm down." A spotlight was shining in her eyes; without turning away, I reached out and switched it off. She was very beautiful. Cornered like that, I found her irresistible. I smiled. "Easy now, easy."

"You're sick!" she shouted at me. She looked at her cell phone. "I'm calling right away if you don't let me out."

I let my gaze linger on her breasts, her hips; this time she didn't have a bag. She finished dialing and turned her back on me. It was perfect.

"Hello! I need help!" she said to the device.

"This is a basement, *señorita*. There's no signal. But you're safe with me. Give me back the books and you can go. I've got a list here of all the others you've stolen, all the books I let you steal, I don't know why."

"Yeah? Why did you? Let me out!" she shouted, but not all that loudly.

"You may not believe this, but there are video cameras here and here and over there," I said, indicating arbitrary points on the ceiling. "I have proof."

"Are you serious?" Now I could discern a slight Argentine or Uruguayan accent, which she had been effectively disguising up till then. "I couldn't see them." She smiled. "I'm sorry. Will you forgive me?"

"Forgive you? Come on! You can start by giving me back the books."

She drew one of the little Russian volumes from each of her armpits and another from her trousers. With a slight but jaunty swing to her hips, she walked confidently across to the shelf from which she had taken the books and put them back.

"There," she said brazenly.

"And the others?"

"Shall we forget them?" she hazarded.

"No, let's think of it as an outstanding debt, a personal loan from me to you. I have partners in this business, you know." I pressed the button to raise the grille and let her out.

She almost ran. I just had time to ask her name before she disappeared up the stairs.

"Call me Ana!" she cried.

I told myself that she'd be back. Suddenly I felt very alone among all those books. I wished the cameras had been real.

■

Bookshops are infested with ideas. Books are quivering, murmuring creatures. That's what one of my business partners used to say. He was a poet, quite a clever guy (though not as clever as he thought), and likable enough. There's something to it: the three little Russian books stood there on the shelf next to the cash register for several days, murmuring, quivering, preserving her memory, but she didn't return. Those were eventful days, or rather I heard that they'd been eventful (there was a rash of lynchings in the inland villages and a coup in a neighboring country, cocaine became the world's number one illicit substance, stagnant water was discovered on Mars, and Pluto definitively lost its status as a planet), my life having shrunk once more to the ambit of books; I had become another specimen of that sad type, the bookseller with literary aspirations.

■

All sorts of people came to visit us every day. Poets, students, lawyers, ladies with or without bodyguards, successful people (economically speaking) and failures (of all kinds). We served them calmly and politely. Sometimes they bought a book or two. Thanks to the new security systems, very few people make a habit of stealing books these days. More than half of them, in my experience, are women or literary types with backpacks or satchels.

I worked at the bookstore on Mondays, Wednesdays, and Thursdays; the rest of the week I spent writing (or fantasizing about it) and reading.

■

The next time I saw her, it was in the street. She was wearing jeans, a short embroidered blouse, white sneakers, and sunglasses. Her hair was tied in a ponytail. My heart began to thump, and I felt a fluttering in my stomach, as you do when you unexpectedly see someone you are strongly attracted to. I started walking quickly to catch up, and when she stopped to wait for the light on the corner of Trece and Reforma, I went and stood beside her.

"Hi. Found you at last."

She looked at me, smiling.

"Ah, it's you."

"Taking a walk?"

"Uh-huh."

The lights changed. We crossed the street.

"Can I come along for a bit?"

"If you like."

We walked for a while in silence. She set a quick pace.

"Can I ask you something?"

She threw me a wary sidelong glance. "You can ask."

"What do you do with the books?"

"Look," she said, "I'm grateful to you for not getting me into trouble the other day, but that's a question I'd rather not answer. It's personal, OK?"

We walked on in silence.

"OK. But now I'm more curious than ever."

There was no reaction from her.

"Are you going somewhere in particular?"

"No," she said as we turned the corner into Séptima. "I just felt like a walk."

On we went.

It was a cool morning; the asphalt and the grass were still wet from the rain overnight. There seemed to be more grackles in the trees than usual.

"Those birds make such a racket," she said.

"It's the season. They're mating."

She looked at me. I think she was impressed by my ornithological knowledge. "Are you interested in birds?"

"I'm interested in most things."

She nodded impatiently.

"Do you live on your own?"

"Yes. Well, no. I live with my father."

I hadn't been expecting that. We took a few more steps in silence.

"How old's your father?"

The smile that spread across her face seemed to be laden with sadness. "He's very, very old."

"Eighty?"

"Are you always so nosy?"

"I'm not, actually. Do you live round here?"

"Stop, will you?"

"Sorry. No more questions." A few moments later, I asked: "Am I bothering you tagging along like this?"

"No, no. Not at all," she said indulgently.

We were on Quinta by this stage. We turned left and then left again.

"Why *are* you tagging along like this?"

I answered without thinking: "I find you attractive."

"That's what I thought. You're not the first, you know."

We had stopped in front of a blue metal door with a little sign that read: *Pensión Carlos.*

"This is where I live," she said. She held out her hand, smiling. "Goodbye."

She turned away, and her profile looked so hard I felt a sharp pain in my stomach.

■

From then on, my days began to gravitate around the Pensión Carlos. I made a detour past it on the way to and from the bookstore; on my days off, I took breaks from writing and went for walks that always ended up leading me, by a more or less circuitous route, back to that calm and shady street. But I didn't run into her again, until one Monday afternoon she reappeared at the bookstore.

She looked radiant in a canary-yellow dress; her skin was deeply tanned, with a subtle moist sheen from some kind of cream, and her thick black hair hung loose on her broad shoulders. As she came in she took off her sunglasses and greeted me with a smile and a resonant "Hi."

I felt an electric current running through me, quickening my blood, along with the usual fluttering. "Welcome back. I thought I wouldn't see you again."

"How are things?" She walked up to the cash register and stood there in front of me, still smiling. "I came for the reading. Am I very early?"

I looked at the clock on the wall.

"The reading's at six. No, you're not too early."

There was a guy browsing, a guy I detested for no particular reason, apart from the fact that he existed, even though he was one of our best clients and bought three books a month on average. Permanently burdened with jacket, tie, and halitosis, he was an economist and a lawyer, and he wrote a weekly column for one of the local newspapers. I wished he would clear out, and as if under the power of a magic spell, he put the volume he was holding back on the shelf and headed for the door, unhurriedly, reading the titles of some of the new books laid out on the tables. Eventually he left, but not before glancing at me with his little ratty—or foxlike—eyes.

"Is this the program?" she said, pointing to a poster stuck on a column beside the cash register. "Blue-eyed poets, eh?"

"It was their idea."

"OK." She tilted her head; she didn't seem convinced. "Are they good?"

"I'm no expert. They're poets. They have their moments, or their instants, anyway."

She laughed. "All right, I'll stay."

"They won't be long." I shut the book I was holding.

"What are you reading?" she asked me.

"Kenko, aphorisms."

"Can I see?"

I handed her the book. She opened it at random, somewhere in the middle.

She read: "It is best not to change something if changing it will not do any good."

"Well, that seems obvious," she said.

"Aphorisms often do, don't they?"

"How about this one: 'The priest known as the Burglar Bishop lived near Yanagihara. His frequent encounters with burglars gave him the name, I understand.'"

"It doesn't seem like an aphorism."

She went on: "It is unattractive when people mingle in a society which is not their habitual one, whether it is an easterner among people from the capital, a man from the capital who has gone east to make his fortune, or a priest of either an exoteric or esoteric sect who has left his original faith."

She closed the book and handed it back to me. She seemed disappointed. "That's really just a prejudice," she said, and I agreed.

"It was written in the fourteenth century. What can you expect?"

"It's still a prejudice," she said, "the way stupidity is always stupid."

I smiled again. "You're pretty severe."

"I'm one of those people who likes to mingle in a society that is not my habitual one," she replied.

"Then Kenko was wrong, because it's hard to imagine a more attractive person than you."

Her expression changed. Now she looked like a little girl who had just done something extremely clever.

"Thank you," she said, looking into my eyes, her head lowered slightly and her shoulders slightly hunched.

■

The blue-eyed poets arrived: seven young people, three of each sex and one of both. They read. Only one of them had any "moments"; the thief and I agreed about that. Otherwise the reading—as a lucid but envious critic later wrote—was as mechanical as a washing machine. The "blue eyes" were ironic; the poets wore colored contact lenses.

When it was over, I returned to the cash register, and she went to join the audience and the poets at the bar that we'd set up in the reading space. I saw her leaf through two or three of the little blue chapbooks that the poets had put on sale for the occasion—produced with greater taste and care than the texts they contained, as the critic was to write—and I guessed that she would take one without paying.

I was glad she stayed when I said I was closing the store. I was putting some copies of the little blue book on the table where we displayed curiosities. She came over.

"You didn't take one, then?"

"You can search me," she said.

"Really?"

She nodded, and all my blood went rushing to one place.

I reached out with my index finger extended and held it half an inch from the red button that worked the security grille.

"Close it," she said.

I pressed the button and the grille came down noisily.

When it was quiet, I asked her to lift up her arms, and she obeyed. We were face to face. I ran my hands gently over her sides, frisking her as I supposed a security professional would, in a methodical and conscientious way, from top to bottom, from bottom to top.

"Satisfied?" she asked.

I didn't laugh. "Well, actually, no." My voice faltered.

"Would you like to continue?" she asked.

"Yes."

"Go ahead."

"Really?"

"Yes, stupid, really!"

I stood behind her and ran my hands over her neck, her back, her legs, which she spread cooperatively, and finally over her buttocks and the inside of her thighs.

"Satisfied now?"

I didn't say anything. Feeling slightly dizzy, I stood up with a difficulty that wasn't affecting my body so much as my will, and came round to face her again.

She gave me a slap, a fairly gentle slap.

"You like to take advantage, don't you?" She smiled and I understood that I had been given permission to kiss her. So I did.

■

"Stop," she said. "Let's stop."

"Why?"

"That's enough," she laughed joyfully. "You're insatiable."

"In this particular case, I am." I ran my hand over my stomach. "And really hungry too. Will you have dinner with me?"

"Sure. I haven't been to a restaurant for ages."

We went up from the basement into the street, where a cold wind was blowing as if from above, like a very fine drizzle.

"Shall we walk?" I took her hand.

"You make me laugh," she said. "Sure, let's walk."

When I saw her shivering, I gave her my jacket.

She stopped and said: "You're very kind, or you seem to be. But life is shit. We better get the car so you can take me back to the *pensión*."

"But why? Why do you say life is shit?"

"Because it's so complicated."

"You're right about that."

"Will you take me back?"

"Do I have a choice?"

We walked to the parking lot in silence and drove slowly, in silence, to the *pensión*. When I was dropping her off, I said: "I'd like to meet your father, if I can."

A bitter smile twisted her mouth. She stood there for what seemed a very long time without speaking. "I don't think it's appropriate," she finally replied.

We didn't set a date to meet. It was as if we had come to a tacit agreement that we would see each other again. I didn't know how many days I'd have to wait; I really didn't think it would be many—and it wasn't, but they seemed endless. One Saturday afternoon in mid-October, after a long debate with myself, I made up my mind to knock on the door of the Pensión Carlos. I'd been obsessed by the thought of her father for some time, and I expected to find him there. At first I imagined a frail and sickly man, perhaps to make sense of the fact that he was living with his daughter in a rented room. He's an invalid, I thought. A sad case. A nobody. Then it occurred to me that he could also be a shady character, someone whom caution or shame had driven into hiding. A washed-up politician? A defrocked priest? A drug boss on the run? An artist?

It was one of those old-fashioned doorbells: a little white button in the middle of a tile. It made a sound that opened passages in my memory, all the way back to a long-forgotten place from my childhood.

A maid in uniform came to the door.

She was still a child, but there was a hardness in her face, which reminded me of the ugly look that country kids take on when, from one day to the next, they become soldiers. Beyond the garage, which was empty, I could see a modern, single-story house, with wrought-iron bars in the windows.

"Who are you looking for?" she asked. "What do you want?"

"Is the *pensión* open?"

She nodded curtly.

"The rooms are rented by the week."

I stood there for a moment looking at the little front garden, with its big pots of Mexican geraniums, sword ferns, aspidistras, and aloe vera.

"Can I see a room?"

"Come in," said the girl, and opened the door that she had been keeping half closed.

The tiles on the floor of the little vestibule, decorated with the signs of the zodiac, the little sitting room with its old sofas and weary armchairs, the wrought-iron bars in the big window that looked onto a shady patio: all this reminded me again of my childhood. Beyond the sitting room, a dimly lit corridor led to the bedrooms and, at the end, a bathroom, from whose open door emerged a powerful odor of household disinfectant scented with apple and eucalyptus, a combination that also triggered early memories. The girl opened the door of the first bedroom and invited me to inspect it. It was a medium-size room, with a window looking out into a garden densely shaded by an old rubber tree. The bed, made of dark wood with carvings of hunting scenes, was high and narrow. I tested the mattress; to my surprise, it was firm. Against the wall opposite the window there was a camp bed, whose presence intrigued me. The maid must have noticed my surprise, because she explained:

"There's an extra charge if you want bedclothes and a pillow for the camp bed."

There were thick Momostenango rugs on the floor, which was tiled, as in the vestibule, but here the tiles were decorated with birds in flight. The only modern object in the room was a chrome-plated reading lamp on the cheap pine bedside table. I switched it on, saw that the light was good, and switched it off again.

"How many rooms do you have?"

"Six."

"How many are free?"

"Just this one."

"I'll take it, then."

She told me the price, which seemed reasonable. After paying a deposit and putting away the receipt she handed me, I said I'd be back that night or the following morning with my things.

■

It wasn't the first time I had let a bookish impulse carry me beyond the bounds of reason. On the way home I kept laughing at myself, thinking of Flaubert. I had been impetuous before: when I got together with my friends to set up a bookstore; when I decided to become a writer; when I ran away from the family home; when . . . but this was different: for the first time in my life, I was embarking on a purely sentimental adventure.

The Pensión Carlos, which I moved into that afternoon, was a quiet place—except at dusk, when a multitudinous flock of grackles darkened the sky and filled the air with their cries. Lying in the darkness I could tell by the electric clock flashing on the bedside table that it was nine. I heard the heavy steps of a man in the corridor, then a woman's heels, a door opening and closing. With my heart beating slightly faster than normal, I got up from the bed and went to the door to listen, but I couldn't hear anything more.

I went back to bed and reread a couple of poems by Darío.

Executioners of ideals have afflicted the Earth,
mankind is imprisoned in a well of darkness
along with the violent mastiffs of hatred and war.

At midnight I switched off the lamp and closed my eyes.

■

I woke up very early. There wasn't much light in the sky, but birds were beginning to stir in the rubber tree outside the window; it took me a few seconds to recognize the room. I lay there for a while, watching the shadows play over the translucent folds of the curtain, as it swayed in the morning breeze. I remembered the dream I'd had a few minutes before—I was being chased by a snake with a body as thick as a horse's—and noticed a strange yet familiar taste in my mouth. "The extra-temporal essence of our lives," I said aloud.

I spent a few more minutes in bed, in a position that favors and symbolizes indolence: hands clasped under my head, feet crossed, ears at once occupied and idle.

Someone went into the bathroom at the end of the corridor and opened a faucet. A dog barked, a motorbike drove noisily down the street.

I got up and opened my suitcase. I took out a pair of trousers, a shirt, and underwear. I was imagining my next encounter with . . . Ana? I wasn't even sure I knew her real name. We would see each other in the corridor, or in the little vestibule, or perhaps outside the *pensión*, in that narrow, shady street.

In fact, we saw each other next at the bookstore. It was Monday. She arrived shortly before the reading, like the other times. The guest that day was my friend Jean Latouche, a French poet. When she came in I was talking with him. I broke off the conversation, excused myself, and went to say hello.

"I'm very glad you came. I've been wanting to see you for days."

"Have you?"

I wondered if she knew that I'd moved into the *pensión*; I hoped not.

"I tried to find you a couple of times."

"Where?" she asked, surprised.

"At the *pensión*."

"Why?"

"I wanted to see you, that's all."

"Ah." She looked me in the eye. "I wanted to see you too."

"Really?"

She nodded. I took her face in my hands and gave her a kiss on the mouth.

"You don't waste any time," she said. "But look . . ." She glanced over my shoulder. "I think someone wants to talk to you."

It was Latouche. He needed to test a microphone, he said. I went with him to the reading space, plugged in some cables, and when I came back to see what she was doing, I realized with a stab of frustration that she had gone.

I rushed to the door and down the corridor, ran up the stairs, but she had disappeared. I returned to the bookstore. My head was spinning. A premonition sent me back to the shelf beside which I had kissed her, and I discovered that she had taken another book: a hardcover edition of Faulkner's *The Wild Palms*, translated by Borges. Rather than anger, I felt a strange relief. I went to the cash register and added Faulkner's novel to the list of stolen books.

I called one of my business partners and asked him to come and take over at the store; there was no way I could stay there for the reading. It would be all right, he said, I could leave; he'd be there within the hour.

Latouche, who had noticed my attempt to slip away discreetly, called out just as I was heading for the door and gave me an inquisitive look. I traced a little circle in the air to signify that we would see each other later on, and went out into the corridor.

It was already dark outside. On Séptima, a team of council workers had opened up the sewers, releasing their stench along with a smell of damp earth. The lighting was poor and at one point I almost fell into a recently dug trench. I kept walking hurriedly toward the *pensión*, although I was sure that I wouldn't find her there.

When I arrived, I went to my room to change my shoes and trousers, which were muddy from the dug-up avenue, and after a moment's consideration I decided to go and talk to the man who was on duty at reception. Pretending that I had some foreign friends coming to visit, I asked if there was a room available. The *pensión* was fully booked, he assured me. That was why she and her father hadn't been able to stay there, I guessed.

"I'll be checking out tonight," I said to the receptionist.

"It's up to you, sir. But I'm afraid a refund won't be possible," he pointed out. "The rooms are rented by the week, as you know."

"That's all right. One question, though. Two weeks ago a young lady was here with her father. Do you know who she was?"

"A young lady with her father? Her name?"

"Ana."

"Her surname?"

"I don't know."

"Well no, sir, no young lady has stayed here with her father this week, as far as I can remember."

I nodded, but didn't believe him.

"Will you be checking out?"

"Not straight away, but yes, I think I'll be leaving tonight."

"As you please," he said with a mysterious smile, which I found disturbing.

I left the *pensión*. In the street, I stopped and hesitated for a moment, then headed back to the bookstore, taking a detour to avoid the muddy avenue.

So had she lied to me about living with her father? Did she live alone? Or with someone who could pass for her father? These questions and various images swirled around in my head. There's no point going on with this, I told myself; it's madness, delirium, and the best thing you can do is forget all about her. Now! But the questions and the images kept preying on my mind, and all that night I don't believe a single minute passed without me thinking of her.

The reading was still going on when I got back to the bookstore. Latouche was a good reader. The last two poems, which I was able to hear in their entirety, drew enthusiastic applause from the audience, but I was there and not there, alien to it all. I was floating in a world whose elements were ill-defined, nebulous, and possibly evil. The idea of hiring a detective to discover her real identity crossed my mind. And it calmed me down, though not for long. In the end, I mixed with the crowd and had a drink.

■

"She'll never forgive you," said Latouche, laughing, when I explained my idea of hiring a detective. "That is, if she finds out. There's no reason why she should, but I know you: you'll end up telling her yourself. You've got it worse than Tristan, my friend! It's obvious. But don't worry; she'll be back. She's already come back twice, or three times, is it? She'll come back again. They always do. Well," he corrected himself, "almost always. The women I've known, anyway."

We drank a lot. Beyond a certain point, most of what we said and did that night was lost to memory. When I got into a cab after saying goodbye to Latouche, I told the driver to go to my apartment; I didn't even think of returning to the *pensión*, and I would regret it the next day.

When I woke up, I didn't recognize my bedroom; for a moment I thought I was at the *pensión*. Then came the sketchy memories of the night before that linger in a brain too liberally flushed with alcohol.

■

"The young lady you were asking about yesterday," said the receptionist at the Pensión Carlos, "she was waiting for you here all last night, sir. She left with her luggage less than an hour ago."

"But you told me there wasn't any young lady . . ."

"But, sir, I can't just give out information about our guests. You didn't know her name. That made me wonder what was going on."

"Whose luggage did you say she left with?"

"Hers, sir. No one has been into your room."

I went to my room, shut the door, and checked that all my things were still there. I sat on the edge of the bed with my head in my hands and my eyes on the floor. That's what I was like when I fell helplessly in love, which is why I'd learned to avoid it. Too late, again, I thought. I had to find her.

I got to my feet, determined to take action. I picked up my suitcase, opened it on the bed, and started collecting my belongings. And that was when I realized that, in spite of what the receptionist had said, someone had come into my room. *She* had. The books that I had brought but barely leafed through since I'd been there—with the exception of the Darío—had disappeared: *Hadrian the Seventh* by Frederick Rolfe, *Interludio azul* by Pere Gimferrer, *Babilonia* by Salvator Rosa, *The Golden Earth* by Norman Lewis, *Espérame en Siberia, vida mía* by Jardiel Poncela. . . . I finished packing and went to talk with the receptionist.

"I don't want to make trouble for you, but someone went into my room."

"Well, yes, they had to clean the room."

"What I meant was, someone went in and took my books."

"Books?"

"Listen." I looked at him as calmly as I could. "Strange as it may seem, this young lady is my friend. That's right, even though I don't know her surname. I haven't known her for long, but we have become friends."

The guy looked at me mischievously.

"It's not what you think. I'm not saying the young lady stole those books from me. But I'm sure she took them. It's a kind of game we've been playing since we met."

"I understand, I think," he said. "But will you be staying or leaving, sir?"

"I'm leaving. But first, I have a question. Were you here when she left? Do you know where she was going?"

"No, sir."

"Was she on her own?"

His annoyed frown indicated that I was harassing him with my questions.

I put a hundred quetzal note on the counter. He shook his head in disapproval but reached out, took the note, and slipped it into his pocket.

"She was with a gentleman."

I felt an unpleasant dizziness, accompanied by strong palpitations.

"Her father?"

He smiled condescendingly.

"He was an older man, yes. But to judge from the names, he

wasn't her father. He was traveling with a lot of books, though. Two suitcases full, plus his personal effects."

"Do you mean she was with him last night?"

"No, sir. Last night the young lady was alone. The old man came to get her and her luggage this morning."

The register was on the counter, open at a blank page. I read the date, upside down. I reached out, spun the book around and turned to the previous page. The second-to-last line read: *Ana Severina Bruguera.* Occupation: *unemployed.* Nationality: *Honduran.* And underneath: *Otto Blanco. Traveler. Spanish.*

"Did he go with her?"

The man looked at me with renewed contempt, and replied with a slight shake of his head. He took hold of the book, closed it, and put it away under the counter.

"As I said, I can't be giving this kind of information out to all and sundry. But if you're interested, I think they were going to the airport."

I thanked him and took my suitcase out into the street, where I hailed a cab.

"You're lucky," said the driver. "I've just come from the airport, and there's not much traffic. It can be hell at this time of day."

If what the receptionist had told me was true, I thought, if she really had left the *pensión* just an hour ago and was heading for the airport, I had a chance of catching her there. I felt that if I let her escape this time I'd lose her forever. "One cannot lose what one does not possess," I said to myself, but it didn't make me feel any better. Maybe she was called Ana Severina Bruguera. Maybe not.

Near the statue of Tecún Umán (the hero of our national history, in spite of the fact that he didn't exist) with his rusted iron spear and his colossal comic-book chest, I realized that it was lucky I had a suitcase with me, because for some time access to the airport had been restricted to passengers. The fact that our international airport is located in the middle of the city says a lot, but on this occasion I was glad of it. Thanks to the suitcase, I got in without any trouble. I went from queue to queue, scanning the passengers lined up to check in at the counters of the foreign and local airlines.

Nothing.

Finally I saw her at the cashier's desk where the airport taxes are collected. Her boarding pass had just been stamped and she had turned to walk toward the automatic glass doors beyond which, without a passport, I wouldn't have been able to follow her. Behind her were two men of different ages. They were engaged in a heated discussion. The older man, who was tall and corpulent, with sparse white hair and pale skin, was loftily looking down at his interlocutor from a height of about six feet. At first I didn't recognize the other, much younger man, who was thin, with jet black hair and a beard, and who turned out to be a colleague, Ahmed al Fahsi, a Moroccan who had a bookstore in La Antigua. Ahmed was a self-declared atheist, but with his Muslim father, Jewish ancestors on his mother's side, and a thorough knowledge of Christian (and Lacanian) doctrine, he came closer than anyone I knew to the model of the "God-fearing man."

Even if I'd broken into a run, I don't think I would have been able to reach her before she went on through the security gate. I could have called out, but I wasn't sure of her name. I stopped.

The man I took to be Otto Blanco showed his papers to the officers and went through the gate, while Ahmed said something to him in a loud voice. A farewell in Hebrew? His brow still furrowed with anger, Ahmed turned, and our eyes met, but I don't think he recognized me and I looked down. We passed each other, coming quite close, as he headed for the exit and I walked toward the cashier's desk, where I turned around, pretending to have forgotten something. A few moments later, I left the airport and, with a tightness in the chest (or was it a gaping hole?), with "death in my soul" as Latouche would have said, I took a cab back home.

—

"It is impossible to be wise and to love at the same time," someone has rightly said.

At first I thought that knowing she was far away would help me forget her. It took me some time to realize that I was mistaken.

That night I had dinner with Latouche, who was flying back to France the next day. I talked about her again, but without mentioning the books I'd let her steal—I didn't want to seem a fool. I remembered that Latouche also knew Ahmed, who at some point had invited him to read at his bookstore. I said that I'd seen Ahmed at the airport, arguing with the putative father of Ana Severina Bruguera.

"And you didn't talk with him? Why not? Though I guess it would have been embarrassing. If I were you, I'd go and see him," said Latouche.

After dinner he asked me to take him to a striptease show that one of my partners had recommended. I said I'd take him there but that I wasn't in the mood for watching the show. He gave up on the idea.

"Let's go to a bar and have a drink, then," he said.

We drank a fair bit, though not as much as the previous night.

"You need to talk to Ahmed," he insisted when we were saying goodbye in front of his hotel.

■

"There's no money for the famine in Africa, but there's money to send satellites into space," Ahmed was saying on the telephone when I walked into his bookstore at the end of Sucia Street in La Antigua. He didn't see me straight away. "Do you know how long it is since it rained in Zagora? Zagora's the town I come from. Yes, in the desert. Fifteen years. That's right, fifteen years!"

He hung up and stared at the old telephone for a while

before lifting his gaze to find out who had come into his store and made the bell ring.

"Ah." He smiled when he saw me. "What's up with the competition?"

"Right, the competition." I looked around. Alfarabi, as his bookstore was called, had many things in common with La Entretenida. "Lucky you're here and we're in the capital."

We shook hands, although, like many Moroccans, Ahmed simply held his hand out and let me do all the shaking. Then he touched his chest, as is customary in his country. I did the same as a reflex or a courtesy or . . . I don't really know why.

"What brings you here? Still chasing tourists?"

I laughed. "Those days are over."

"Not yet, surely?"

"No, I mean it."

"How's business?"

"It's OK, amazingly enough. I always think most people read very little, if they read at all. And yet there are some who buy quite a few books, thank God."

"Yes." Ahmed smiled. "*Hamdul-lah!* Look." He showed me a book with a black cover, from the Tusquets New Sacred Texts list. "Have you read it?"

It was Jorge Riechmann's *Conversations Between Alchemists*, and I hadn't read it.

"It's not bad," said Ahmed, "for a Spaniard."

There might be something else in the mix, with a name like that, I thought. But I didn't want to argue.

"Here, it's a present." He handed me the book. "See what you think."

"Thank you. Are you sure?"

"Of course."

Ahmed wasn't in the habit of giving away books. I thought, unfairly, that it must be very bad. I looked at the price on the back; it was worth a simple lunch for two.

"Let's go eat somewhere. My treat."

Ahmed accepted, and a few moments later we left the store and started walking up Sucia Street to the arcades around Parque Central.

"This part of La Antigua," said Ahmed, "reminds me of Ksar-el-Kebir."

"I can't really see why, but then, why not?" I must have been in a good mood; Ksar had always seemed a horrible place to me. "I guess they're both old colonial cities."

We sat down at an iron table on the patio of a restaurant, and I opened Riechmann's book at random.

"We have no money . . ." I read. "So this book made you think of me, did it, Ahmed?"

"Maybe, maybe not. But the way I see it, you and I, we're like alchemists."

I didn't quite understand his reasoning, but I was inclined to agree with him.

"So," he said after a while, "what's the mystery?"

"There actually is a mystery that I think you could help me solve."

He raised his eyebrows. He looked puzzled. I guess he was amused by my declaration.

"OK then," he said.

I didn't want to give it all away, partly because I was worried that there might have been something between Ahmed and Ana, as there had been between Ana and me. So I passed over the erotic aspect of the story, concentrated on the stolen books, and finished with a little embellishment: I told Ahmed that I'd seen him with Ana and Señor Blanco at the airport when I was going to catch a flight to Flores.

"Who was the old man?"

"It's her husband," he said, and sat there watching me with a blank expression. Then his dark, narrow eyes sparkled with something that I took to be a hint of mockery. "Did you think he was her father? Well, he's not. If you ask me, it's what they call a marriage of convenience."

He had noticed the effect of his words. My hands were shaking slightly.

"I had no idea. I'd rather she was single, I admit."

"Did she steal many books from you?"

"Quite a few. To tell the truth, I let her steal them, so I can't really complain."

"It could happen to anyone," he said. "But they're not going to get away with it, not with me, *sidi*. No sir. They owe me a packet, those two. And they're going to pay, I'm telling you. It may take a while, but sooner or later, they'll pay."

"Did you have any dealings with her?"

"Dealings?" Ahmed laughed. "She tried to seduce me, if that's what you mean. Hah!" he said smugly. "That woman is a thief. She stole books from me too. Lots! Too many! I caught her one day with a first edition of Laoust's stories, you know? That's right. A treasure. I called the police. They arrested her. The old guy had to come and buy her out. A bribe, and he paid me cash for the book. He tried to make excuses, saying that she suffered from some kind of illness, that books were the only thing she stole, and that she read them. He asked me to let her come back to Alfarabi and said that he'd pay for anything she took. She didn't know about this arrangement, and he asked me to keep it secret. And so the game began. She knew my hours, and she used to come in the morning, when I wasn't there. She could always fool my employees and she took three or four books each time. I'd arrive at midday, check the shelves to see what was missing, and call her husband, who'd come to pay in the afternoon. The last time she took a lot more books than usual. I don't know how she did it; she must have filled a backpack. I called her hotel, and they told me she'd gone. I gave up on the books, of course. But then I had a stroke of luck. The travel agent who sold them the tickets is a friend of mine. I had told him the story, and since he knew the old guy by sight, he tipped me off. I went to the airport to catch them."

"Did he pay you?"

"In part. He promised they'd be back and gave me an IOU for the rest."

"When are they coming back?"

"In December." He calculated. "Nine months, right?"

A feeling of relief flooded through me: there was still a possibility that I might see her again.

"That's good news. I'll be looking forward to December. Will you let me know if you find out they're back?"

Ahmed laughed before promising:

"Of course, my friend."

■

How many nights did I spend fantasizing about our next encounter? I imagined her traveling from country to country, visiting bookstore after bookstore.

More than once I thought about talking to Ahmed. I wanted to know which books she had stolen from him, apart from the Berber stories. But I was too embarrassed to call.

I kept going over the books that she had taken from me and trying to imagine the complete list of every title she had ever stolen. It was as if I thought this would help solve the mystery of a life that seemed bizarre and fantastic to me.

Ahmed had spoken of an illness. But I felt that there must have been another explanation, which I associated with an uncompromising approach to life: absolute freedom, a radical realization of the ideal that I too had adopted one fine day—the ideal of living by and for books.

There were black days when those fantasies faded away, leaving me prey to despondency and remorse for a life half-lived. I would think: "You're kidding yourself; she's just a common thief, or, at best, a sad case, a kleptomaniac."

One night toward the end of June I dreamed of her. It was a happy dream, a typical dream of making love, devoid of the anxiety that generally infuses dreaming. I woke in the darkness and silence with a pleasant feeling of gratitude, which soon gave way to a sense of loss and absence. I went back to sleep with the vain hope of finding her again in the next dream and wishing, simply and absurdly, that December would hurry up and come.

■

I met other women. I traveled. I read, bought, and sold many books. I celebrated another birthday, and finally December came. I couldn't say I was miserable, but something essential to happiness was certainly missing from my life.

There were readings at La Entretenida on the first two Mondays of the month, and I attended both as if going on a date. I went to bed early the night before, so as not to have bags under my eyes; I did a bit of exercise, put on my best pair of trousers and shoes, my best shirt and jacket. She didn't show, of course. On the fifteenth of December I called Ahmed. He told me he didn't have any news. Because of the New Year vacation, there wouldn't be any more poetry readings until the end of January. I did my best to resign myself to never seeing her again.

I've always been wary of the word *never* and the word *infinite*, for reasons that are, I think, fundamental. But now the two words were touching, so to speak, in the turbulent darkness of my mind.

I dreamed more in my waking hours than when I was asleep. I kept imagining scenes in which we met. I spoke to her straightforwardly. Although I knew that stealing, in her case, was not a symptom but a mode of existence (not that I really knew this), I insisted that with me she could be sure of having a virtually inexhaustible supply of reading material, without having to run any more risks. How long was she going to persist with the sham marriage? Couldn't she leave that fat old husband of hers? And so on. Things I'd never have dared to say if, on one of those dismal days, our paths had actually crossed.

One morning I was out for an aimless stroll when suddenly I realized that I was right near the front door of the Pensión Carlos. I heard a metallic click (a sound that will perhaps be familiar to some of you one day: the tapping of a walking stick on cement), and then I saw old Blanco, the fat guy from the airport, who didn't actually look so old or so fat any more. We passed each other on the sidewalk, barely exchanging glances, without any kind of greeting. He was very tall and ungainly.

I walked a few more steps. To him I was a perfect stranger. But was it really him? I wasn't sure. I stopped; I had to talk to him. I could use the pretext of the books, to begin with. I turned around and was going to say something, but the street wasn't a good place for the kind of conversation I had in mind, so instead of accosting him I rang the bell of the *pensión*.

I took out a card, wrote my telephone number, and signed

my name. The cleaner opened the door. I asked her to give the card to Señor Blanco, and she took it with a grunt.

I went back out into the street just in time to see him turning the corner. Instead of following him, I continued with my aimless stroll, but the relative calm I had enjoyed until that chance encounter was utterly shattered.

This happened on a Monday, I think, but since there wasn't a reading, I opened the bookstore around three.

He was the first person to come in. He wished me a good afternoon.

"Señor Blanco? You got my message?"

He approached the counter unhurriedly.

"I'm Otto Blanco, yes, but I didn't get any message." He smiled.

I told him my name and we shook hands.

"I left my card at your *pensión* a couple of hours ago."

"Ah," he said with a worried look. "Is it to do with Ana?"

Ana, I thought. So she didn't lie to me.

"Yes, but don't worry." I gestured in a way that must have been incomprehensible; it was a kind of involuntary reflex. I laughed. "It has to do with her. I believe she is your . . . wife?"

He frowned.

"Did she say that?"

After an awkward moment, we both smiled.

So was it Ahmed who lied? I wondered.

"Are we talking about the same person? Ana Bruguera?"

"Yes," he replied. "Ana Severina Bruguera Blanco."

"She told me she lived with her father. But excuse me, Señor Blanco, I don't mean to pry."

"I'm her mother's father, her grandfather. But it's true that I've been a father to her, really. And . . ."

Another awkward silence.

"It's about stolen books, isn't it?"

A moment later I was showing him the long list of books that I had stuck to the column next to the cash register. He began to read it slowly, with a look of satisfaction and a new sharpness in his watery eyes.

"We have read all these books together," he said, having reached the end of the list and turned to me. "I didn't know where they came from. I'm sorry. She doesn't tell me everything, you know."

"She's your granddaughter, you say." I couldn't believe it, but I dearly wanted to.

"Won't you dell me how mush we owe you?" Suddenly his accent sounded very strange. Asian or maybe Central European, I thought. It was as if the nerves and muscles supporting his Spanish had momentarily relaxed.

"That's not what I wanted to talk about. Actually, I'd like to see Ana again."

He swallowed and blinked.

"And why would you want to see her?"

The question made me feel like a schoolboy. I wasn't going to tell him that I was in love. I couldn't think of anything to say.

"You're not the first bookseller to fall in love with her," said the old man. "If you change your mind, send the bill to me at the *pensión.*"

"Are you very busy?"

He looked at me blankly.

"Me? I'm an idler, more or less. No, I have nothing at all to do."

I invited him to have a drink in the café on the corner.

"As you can see, it's a slow day here. Just let me shut the store. I'm pretty much an idler myself," I admitted.

We walked in silence to the café. Señor Blanco didn't look at all as I remembered him. He was strongly built, with a broad forehead and a tanned face, although his hands were pale. We both ordered black tea with lemon.

"I ought to begin by pointing out, though it shouldn't come as a surprise, that we're really quite ordinary people. I have my ideas, and she goes along with them, but in her own way, of course. Books have always been my life. Both my father and grandfather lived exclusively from books, each in his way— books of all sorts. And I'm not speaking metaphorically: books are our sole means of subsistence," he said and then fell silent.

"It's very different for me. Neither my father nor my grandparents were interested in books. The only person who read in our house was my mother."

I felt like a neophyte who has just met his master, the guide he needs to reach the source of wisdom.

Señor Blanco looked at me with what I thought was compassion. He continued: "We have been accused of all sorts of vices and misdemeanors, even crimes." (Was that why she had said "Life is shit"? I wondered.) "We have been called secret agents and confidence tricksters; we have been taken for spies using books to transmit coded messages; it has been said that we collect editions or copies of books related to all sorts of crimes and scandals, that we purvey pornography of one sort or another, or what have you. But the only thing we do consistently is use books to make a living. Let me tell you something. One of my uncles—he was crazy, it's true, but he also had moments of genius—believed, or said he believed, that books, the objects that we call books, are animated by a kind of collective spirit. Like machines and computers in science-fiction fantasies, and the plants from which drugs are extracted, and even certain metals, like gold and iron. He talked about how books struggle for domination in certain regions of the planet, a phenomenon whose trends and flows could be tracked using one of those maps with colored arrows to indicate things like the spreading of ethnic groups or languages over the course of history. Migrations, invasions, outbreaks, extinctions. There are wars between different kinds or genres of books, he said. And, as in real wars, the best don't always win; but for us, in the end, there are no losers, although they all fade away. We use these ebbs and flows the way a sailor uses ocean currents. We exploit them as best we can, beyond literary good and evil, so to speak. We, that is, my granddaughter and I, are still navigating the tides and currents of books."

When he came to the end of his speech we sat there for a few minutes in silence, but the communication between us was still going on, and I was beginning to feel very much at ease in the old man's company.

"You're right," I confessed. "I'm like the other booksellers. I've fallen in love with your granddaughter."

His face changed; now he seemed distant and wary.

"I don't know if she's slept with you. If she has, you've reason to be proud. And now, if you'll excuse me . . ." He got to his feet and so did I. "I would have liked to be able to say *mon frère*," he said. "Goodbye."

I sat down again and stayed there, perfectly still, as if I'd been hit on the back of the neck with a blunt instrument, while the unlikely grandfather of Ana Severina Bruguera Blanco receded into the distance and disappeared.

Our unexpected and implausible encounter was to be continued that night in a dream. We were traveling on a mountain road in a rickety old bus.

"But tell me," I said to the old man, "where is she?"

"You won't see her again. Forget her. She's dead. Dead! Do you understand? She was killed by some kids in Montevideo."

I woke with a feeling of emptiness in my chest, and a deep and pervasive sense of ill-being. I thought I was going to vomit.

■

I managed to get to sleep again around midday and woke at dusk, feeling hungry, with a vague memory of the previous evening and just a few loose threads of what had happened that night. After my conversation with Señor Blanco, I had gone back to the store, and a few hours later, tired of waiting for customers, I closed up.

I went to one of the few old-fashioned cantinas left in the part of the city where I lived. It was in a little street from another epoch, made for carts not cars, which sloped down to a wide, modern avenue where the traffic was hindered by street vendors and stands selling fruit and candy along one of the sidewalks. Narrow steps led from the avenue up to the cantina's tiny terrace, where all sorts of drunks congregated. At that hour of the afternoon, the concrete around there gave off a powerful odor of urine, a reek of liquor filtered through the bodies of those nameless men, irresistibly drawn or driven to drink. Sad cases. Old friends of mine, distant relatives, and in-laws had done time in that place.

I walked into the cantina thinking I was no different from the rest of them and drank so much I can only just remember the faces of the men who lurched around me, and a few of their tall tales, and the queue of drunks waiting to piss in a filthy corner where a hole in the wall, barely concealed by a dirty little curtain, had been turned into a urinal.

Somehow I ended up in another place downtown. Night had fallen, and I was sitting at the bar in a very dark room, with grotesque figures daubed on the walls in fluorescent paint. A bald man with a big gut was drinking next to me; he had a mustache and a long thick beard the color of ash, and he was wearing clear spectacles with large round plastic frames.

"I know you. But do you know me? Of course not!" he said and started laughing.

From the little I can remember of our conversation, he was an artist. I think his next project was going to be the production of a "living necklace." He was thinking of making it with street dogs or cats. The idea was to attach a little honey-smeared rubber sphere to a fishing line and get an animal to swallow it. When the sphere, still attached to the line, emerged several hours later from the anus, it would be washed, smeared with honey again and given to the next dog or cat; each animal would become a bead, a "living bauble." This word seemed to amuse him greatly. I don't know how many times he repeated:

"A self-threading bauble, *un bibelot* . . . Brilliant, isn't it?"

I left that dive with the artist and a friend of his who was bragging about being a thief. He specialized in stealing art and antique furniture from old houses in the city center, which he could get into—so he claimed—thanks to his knowledge of a system of sewers that dated back to colonial times. He came from an aristocratic family; he tactfully declined to reveal his surname, but offered his fair skin and light eyes as a guarantee. In his youth he had wanted to be a historian. I can't remember if we took a taxi or walked to the red light district. We went in and out of various clubs where there were girls performing. In one, I watched an acrobatic dancer: she was hanging head down in a metal tube, stripping to the rhythm of a catchy, schmaltzy tune. She looked so like Ana Severina that I asked the waiter to bring her over to our table when she finished her number. I bought her a drink.

■

She's dead. Dead! Señor Blanco had said to me. I woke with a jolt, and it took me a few seconds, sitting on the bed, to convince myself that he had said it in the dream.

It turned out to be one of those black days. Afflicted with a headache and a mood of heavy melancholy, both of which lasted till late afternoon, I couldn't think clearly about anything. I told myself, once again, to forget that elusive woman. At dusk I wrote a note to her supposed grandfather, explaining that I didn't expect any payment for the books she had taken from La Entretenida. All I wanted, I said again, was to stay in touch with his granddaughter. My feelings for her, I assured him, were affectionate but disinterested, and I stressed that I was writing to him in a spirit of the most sincere friendship. Since it wasn't too late when I finished writing the note, I put it in an envelope and set off for the *pensión*.

It was already dark, but the weather was mild for December and there was no wind, so I went on foot. I walked quickly, propelled by a strange optimism, wondering how many times I had passed that way, thinking of her, telling myself that this story had gone on long enough already, that it was time to bring it to an end, but with no sense of what the future might hold regarding affairs of the heart.

It's not an expression I'd normally use, like the words *never* and *infinite*. But in the course of that walk, it occurred to me that the origin of the term *infinite* must have more to do with the heart than with the rational mind. One can conceive of an "infinite desire" or an "infinite longing," but the logical consequences of the notion of infinity are devastating; we are not mentally equipped to grasp the idea of an infinite object, be it infinite in time (eternity) or in space (a limitless physical universe), or even, strictly speaking, in the abstract realm of numbers.

The *pensión* was in a state of chaos. Two men—traveling salesmen, I presumed—were waiting at reception, but there was no one to serve them. The telephone was ringing in vain on the desk. The cleaner was going back and forth with huge piles of dirty sheets and towels, and a few seconds after I came in, an ambulance, siren blaring and lights flashing, pulled up outside the front door with a screech of tires. Instead of leaving the note for Señor Blanco on the desk, I put it away and discreetly took up a position next to the salesmen.

Two paramedics in green uniforms came in with a stretcher, and the cleaner pointed to the door of a guest's room, which had been left ajar. One of the paramedics pushed the door open, and that's when I saw her. I leaned on the counter with one hand, overcome by a dizzy spell and seized by a strong impression of déjà vu. Ana Severina, framed by the door, was facing away from me. She was wearing a violet-colored dress, cut low in the back, almost down to the waist. Her hair was loose, resting on her shoulders. Sensing that the door was opening behind her, she turned. She would have been able to see me, I think, but maybe she didn't recognize me. She spoke to the paramedic who had entered the room and stepped aside so that the other man in green could bring in the stretcher. Then all three of them disappeared behind the door.

"The old guy must have pegged out," said one of the salesmen. "You could tell he wasn't in good shape, and with a babe like that . . ." He looked at his colleague mischievously.

"Good way to go, though. I wouldn't mind," said the other man.

The blood was humming in my ears, but what I felt, more than rage, was contempt for that pair of losers.

"Listen, she's his granddaughter," said the cleaner through her teeth.

A moment later the paramedics emerged with Señor Blanco on the stretcher. His eyes were shut; he seemed to be unconscious. As Ana came out of the room, she saw me.

"Ana!"

"Oh, it's you," she replied, and came over to hug me, while the paramedics put the old man into the vehicle. "Will you come with me?"

Without replying, I accompanied her to the ambulance, and after helping her into the back, where one of the paramedics was putting an oxygen mask over Señor Blanco's face and the other was giving him an injection in the arm, I leaped in too. The driver pulled away abruptly.

"He was sitting on the edge of the bed, and I saw him fall back. He fainted," said Ana. "A stroke, I guess."

"Yes, a stroke, a brain hemorrhage," said one of the paramedics.

For a moment the sound of the siren—which was all I could hear—reminded me of the original sirens, who had the bodies of birds, not fish, and whose song led men to their ruin. The incoherent images that tumbled through my mind left me thinking that the idea of love that comes down to us from the Romantics, who associated it with death and sometimes with the devil, was too gloomy to be credible, much less desirable, these days. Modern love, twenty-first-century love, had to be different, I thought straightforwardly, maybe just to reassure myself.

The old man was breathing with obvious difficulty. I took Ana's hand and squeezed it. Without turning to look at me, without taking her eyes off her grandfather's lifeless form, she returned the pressure. Then she gently removed her hand.

I sensed that the old man was going to die. I imagined the possibility of a gratifying transference: Ana would turn her attention to me.

"He's dying, this time he's dying," she said.

The senior paramedic's gaze was oscillating between his watch and the old man's chest. He said: "He's not in danger; he's breathing normally."

"He's not going to wake up," Ana said to him.

The paramedic didn't reply.

The ambulance accelerated, and thanks to inertia—"beautiful inertia"—Ana pressed against my shoulder. I turned to hold her.

We stayed like that, neither of us saying a word, until we reached the hospital. The ambulance pulled up at the emergency entrance, and the siren stopped.

"I'm terrified of hospitals," said Ana, who seemed diminished, the very image of desolation. "Will you stay with me?"

I helped her out of the ambulance under the hospital's neon sign, while the paramedics transferred Señor Blanco from the stretcher to a trolley. A cold breeze had sprung up. Ana was shivering. She put her arm around my waist, and I put mine around her shoulders, and clasped together like that we walked into the hospital.

"You go with him. I'll take care of the rest." Suddenly I felt like a father, although my feelings for her were far from paternal.

She followed the trolley into the intensive care unit and disappeared behind the swinging doors.

I went to the admissions desk. I filled in the forms and provided the guarantees required for Señor Blanco to be admitted. With a mixture of hope and fear, I imagined the tangle of consequences to come, all traceable to the physical act of writing my name and contact details on that piece of paper and signing it.

■

I sat in the waiting room for just over an hour. An image came to me from something I had read—I can't remember what: a Hindu monk who spent nine years absorbed in meditation, with his face to the wall, in order to discover Nothingness, Nirvana, the extinction of individual existence. I felt stupid: I had just signed papers that committed me to covering the hospital fees of a man I barely knew, the grandfather of a woman I barely knew either, and who—from the little I did know of her—was not exactly what you would call trustworthy. And then, just like that, with a shrug of my shoulders, a deep breath, a change in the contents of my visual field (from the toes of my shoes to a polar bear swimming with her cubs among chunks of ice in blue water on a muted television screen in the waiting room), suddenly I felt deeply in love and ready to stand by the vows that I still hadn't sworn. For the first time in my life I was determined to give love every chance to run its course. I had signed those papers as one might sign a marriage register. And for a moment I felt freed, released from mere appearances and from an ingrained but strange vanity—the obscure vanity of the single man. I told myself that I had taken the first step toward liberation through love.

At eleven-thirty I began to nod off. A siren woke me. In a flurry of controlled agitation, a group of nurses and paramedics surrounded by men armed with machine guns and assault rifles burst into the hospital wheeling a young man on a trolley. The sheet covering his body was soaked with blood. They went into the intensive care unit; two men stayed to guard the door.

At last Ana appeared.

"They say he's stable," she said. "But he has to spend the night here."

"He's stable," I repeated to myself. I was starting to get seriously worried about the hospital bill.

Ana smiled; she had read my mind.

"Keeping him here could work out to be really expensive, couldn't it?"

"Tonight's already paid for, anyway."

"Really? Thank you," she said. "I think we can go now." She swiveled her eyes like a comic actress.

■

Christmas and New Year's went by, and still Señor Blanco hadn't regained consciousness.

During that time, we read or reread the following books, among others:

La tentation d'exister
Contre la musique
La carne, la morte e il diavolo
Daphnis et Chloe
Une ténébreuse affaire
The Honorable Picnic
Plain Pleasures

Black Spring
Among the Cynics
Flirtation
The Book of Heaven and Hell

"You're not going to believe me," said Ana Severina one night—her spirits seemed to be lifting again—"but I was in Borges's library, in 1999, in Buenos Aires."

We were sprawled among books in the living room of my apartment, where we spent most of our time. I propped myself up on an elbow and gave her my full attention.

"His widow wouldn't let anyone in, but she was in Geneva at the time. One way or another I managed to charm the person in charge," Ana explained, rather ambiguously, but I didn't press her for details—I didn't want to spoil the moment—"and I was allowed in, under strict surveillance, of course. Video cameras and everything, like in your bookstore, huh," she joked. "I went back day after day for three straight weeks. The happiest and strangest weeks of my life!"

This made me feel absurdly jealous.

"It was incredible, chaotic, full of treasures," Ana said with a laugh.

She told me about the notes Borges had made in the margins or on the flyleaves of his books: sentences that underpinned or opened or closed some of his most famous essays and stories.

"You might find this hard to believe, but I didn't take anything," said Ana. "I didn't dare!"

For weeks, we talked about that library and others, while Señor Blanco remained in the hospital, in a coma.

Ana Severina had kept the room at the Pensión Carlos, but we ate together once or twice a day, and she often spent the night with me. I ended up giving her a key to my apartment.

I thought of Ahmed occasionally, but during those days of happiness I didn't call him and he didn't call me.

One afternoon, I think it was in March, Ana Severina and I had the following conversation. We were in an old Chinese restaurant.

"There's no point keeping him in the hospital, is there?" she began.

"I wasn't going to say it; I wouldn't have dared. But you're right; I don't think there's anything more they can do for him there."

"We're just throwing money away."

I took her hand, relieved. But straight away I felt burdened with worry again. Now Ana would have to look after her grandfather, I thought. I remembered that *ana* means *I* in Arabic. I felt grateful for the sudden, natural deaths of my parents, years earlier. The motionless ghost of Señor Blanco floated before me in imagination.

"What are you thinking about?" she asked.

"What do you prefer to be called? Ana or Severina? Or . . . ?"

"He used to just call me Severina."

"Severina, then."

■

The doctors agreed that medical science could do nothing more for the comatose old man.

"The best thing would be for us to go back to the *pensión*," Severina said to me.

I disagreed. "Even if you didn't have to pay for the room there, you'd be much more comfortable in my apartment."

"Maybe."

I explained that as well as the bedroom, which she was familiar with, there was a little servant's room beyond the kitchen and the laundry that wasn't being used.

The room was dark. One of the idiosyncrasies of the local architecture is to provide servants not with a room as such but with a kind of wardrobe just big enough to stand in beside a small bed, and a child-size bathroom with a cold-water shower. Still, it seemed to me that it would be sufficient for an old man in a coma.

When I showed Severina the room, it smelled of damp, of stored clothes and old shoes; it hadn't been properly aired for months, maybe years. In one corner there was a broom, a pile of scourers, and a dustpan. I was ashamed.

"All this will go, Severina. I'll have a word to Juana. We have to get rid of this mess."

"Is it the cleaning lady's room? Are you going to kick her out?"

"She only comes in once a week."

"Where's she from?"

"The altiplano, like almost all of them."

"Is she Mayan?"

"Well, yes."

"They scare me, you know, cleaning ladies."

■

She didn't agree with me that her grandfather, in his current state, wouldn't realize what kind of room he was in. But there was no alternative. He'd be too exposed in the living room. He'd be in the way in my bedroom. And there was no space in the little room that I used as a study. I promised that as soon as he recovered consciousness, we'd put him in a more suitable place.

"Do you think he'll wake up one day?" she asked me.

■

A silent ambulance transported us from the hospital to the apartment building. The paramedics took Señor Blanco up in the elevator and, after settling him in the little servant's room, showed us what to do with the serum dispenser and explained some other care procedures.

"It's awful," said Severina when the paramedics had gone. "This was what he feared the most: having to depend on others. We often talked about it. He once said—"

"What?"

"Nothing, nothing."

She looked at him for a while, and I decided to leave them alone. She was clearly in the grip of an inner conflict. A few minutes later she came into the living room.

"You're going to think I'm very selfish," she said. "I hope you won't take this the wrong way."

I guessed what she was going to say from the tortured expression on her face:

"Maybe the best thing to do would be to disconnect that business, don't you think?"

I didn't say yes or no. It would be a very slow death, I thought.

Severina hugged me. Then (the way she had of doing things like this was all her own) she led me to my bedroom, and there, in what had become my own private plot of earthly paradise, we remained, clocking up two or three more hours on the (illusory) meter of my happiness.

■

The cleaning lady used to come on Tuesdays. It was April already, and with the arrival of the dry season's all-withering winds, dust had settled in every nook and cranny of the apartment.

That Tuesday, before going out, Severina came to kiss me in bed. Her damp hair brushed my face. It smelled of almonds.

I got up shortly afterward with a number of premonitions, but they were so vague as to be almost nonexistent. I thought uneasily about Juana, the cleaning lady. I didn't feel like explaining that I had guests. I bolted my breakfast and vacated the kitchen a few minutes before she arrived.

While she washed up in the kitchen and swept the bedroom and the bathroom, I was reading Schnitzler's aphorisms. Finally she moved on to the laundry and the room where Señor Blanco lay.

Her brief, shrill cry made me shudder, even though I'd been anticipating something like that. Then I heard her steps coming from the laundry. She stopped in the doorway between the living room and the kitchen.

"Is he asleep?"

"He's unconscious."

"Out of it? Poor thing."

"We have to look after him."

"Can he hear?"

"I'm not sure."

"Is it like being dead?"

"More or less."

I went on reading and smoking on the divan in the living room. The rhythm of Juana's activity slowed noticeably. Before she left, she asked timidly if the guests would be staying long. I said I didn't know, and to judge from the look on her face, she wasn't happy about that.

■

As I feared—although I hadn't dared articulate my forebodings —it became clear after a few days that I would have to take care of the old man more or less on my own. Severina didn't withhold her favors (or, for that matter, give me any reason to suppose that she wanted to live with me forever), but her absences from the apartment grew longer and longer.

She would come back with new books—often titles I'd never heard of—and there was almost always an extraordinary discovery among them, or so it seemed to me. We persisted in the pleasant habit of reading together, quietly, each in a corner with our different books, sometimes for whole afternoons or evenings, occasionally exchanging remarks or reflections, ranging from the vague to the penetrating, on the books or on life in general.

"Pay no heed to those dissimilar sisters, Admiration and Envy, daughters of Merit, the false friend of Success," she read.

"Who's that?"

"I don't know," she replied. "Someone wrote it in the margin." She closed the book to show me the cover. It was *On Neoclassicism* by Mario Praz.

I made a sign to ward off the evil eye.

"It's funny," said Severina. "It looked like a new book."

■

She used to wake at dawn. The first thing she would do, after taking a shower and getting dressed, was check her grandfather's serum. Then she'd eat a quick breakfast and go out. When the cleaning lady was coming, she'd stay out for lunch. She seemed to be genuinely afraid of people who cleaned the houses of others. One day I asked her if she could tell me why.

"They can know all about you, but you don't know anything about them."

I was thinking: that's what our relationship is like.

"You're right." Again, I felt she was reading my mind.

"It's what happens when a relationship is based on necessity," she said.

"Yes, when it's like that, there's nothing you can do."

We laughed breezily.

"I hope it's not a bother for you, Papa occupying that room."

"Papa? No, not really."

"I used to call him Papa sometimes," she said, and then looked thoughtful. "We're making your life complicated, aren't we?"

"Just a bit. But I'm not complaining." *Yet*, I added silently.

"Not yet," she said.

"Your father, sorry, your grandfather can stay here as long as necessary or until you decide otherwise, all right?"

■

Señor Blanco was lying still, his face relaxed, his mouth slightly open, as the mouths of the old often are when they sleep, and the slow, gentle rise and fall of his chest as he breathed seemed normal.

"Señor Blanco?"

Nothing.

I approached the bed. Very gently, I prodded his shoulder.

Nothing.

I leaned over him and blew on his face, slightly disgusted by the greasy odor he gave off, but feeling a certain tenderness toward him.

Nothing.

After carefully examining that enigmatic, defenseless body once again, I reached out and gave him a quick, hard pinch below the nipple.

Nothing.

I stayed there for a while, looking at the transparent bag of serum. "Dextrose solution," I read. I examined the little tube, the dropper.

■

I flopped back onto the divan to read and smoke, but not as calmly as before.

"Maybe the real problem," I found myself thinking, "would be if Señor Blanco opened his eyes." The thought had crossed my mind before, but never quite so vividly.

In a way, though, I would have liked him to wake up, because my greatest fear was that his disappearance would upset the balance of my relationship with Severina, which, I was ashamed to admit, depended to some degree on the old man's state of unconsciousness. The last thing I wanted was any kind of change.

Although it would have been easy to end his life, I persuaded myself that I shouldn't: I might never find another source of information like him. And such a man, I thought, is more needful in this world than in the other, as Georg Christoph would have said. I couldn't go on reading. I smoked a cigarette or two. I fell asleep. I was woken by the sound of the door opening and Severina's silvery voice calling out, "I'm home."

No way am I going to kill her grandfather, I thought. I got up to greet her and gave her a kiss and a welcoming hug.

She showed me the afternoon's haul of books.

La española inglesa
Flight from a Dark Equator
The Way of All Flesh
Carnets d'Afrique
Le Poisson-scorpion

"You've brought me luck," she said.

"Why do you say that?"

"Do you realize, since I've been with you, I haven't got caught once?"

"Let's hope it continues that way."

I wondered how the conversation would have gone if I'd decided to kill her grandfather.

Later, while we were having dinner, she said, "Something's bothering you, isn't it?"

I denied it.

"You look worried," she insisted. "Is it my grandfather?"

"Well, yes." I was convinced that she could read my thoughts.

"Are you fed up?"

"No. But I am worried."

She was quiet for a while.

I thought: It's strange. From her expression, I can tell what she's about to say. She's going to suggest that we let her grandfather go.

"I've been thinking," she said a moment later. "Maybe the best thing for everyone, including him, would be for us to let him die."

We looked at each other for a moment in silence.

"Maybe," I said finally.

She nodded and went on eating.

■

La Entretenida was flourishing. But I had begun to feel that there was something crass about simply trading books for money. I was increasingly bored at the store, even when there was a reading, in spite of the new grouplets of poets organizing more or less provocative events for the benefit of a more or less demanding public. Severina, of course, refrained from attending.

The idea of selling my share of the bookstore became more and more attractive, especially since I had borrowed money to pay Señor Blanco's hospital bill, and the interest was accumulating rapidly. In order to test the water with my partners, I said I was thinking of traveling for a few months. They wanted to know where and why.

"I'm not sure. Somewhere calm and not too expensive. Costa Rica? Ecuador? I want to try my luck at writing a novel. If I don't do it now, when will I?"

They began to tease me and I realized that they knew about Severina and her unconscious grandfather staying in my apartment. I didn't try to discover the source of the leak.

"You've really fallen for her; come on, admit it."

"But who could blame you? Such a pretty name: Severina."

I tried to laugh with them. "Well, like I said, I'm ready to sell whenever you want."

One afternoon, when I returned to the apartment, I found her sitting at the kitchen table. She had her head in her hands and didn't look up when I greeted her. I leaned down to kiss her on the back of the neck; she didn't react.

"What's up?"

With a movement of her head she indicated the servant's room, and I understood that Señor Blanco had died. Without saying anything more, I went to the door and saw what I knew I would see: his old lifeless body. "I'm going to miss him," I thought. And then: "Am I really?"

I went back to the kitchen, and it was only then that I saw a plastic bag from the supermarket scrunched up on the table. Suddenly the image of Severina suffocating her grandfather appeared before my eyes. Letting him starve would have been much worse. "She did the right thing," I thought.

"I'm sorry." I sat down at the table opposite her; she still hadn't said anything. Then she looked up with a strange grimace on her face: a smile twisted by sorrow, but only on one side. She shut her eyes and opened them again.

"Thank you," she said. "You understand, don't you?"

"What do you think we should do now?"

"I don't know."

I stood up, walked around the table, leaned over Severina, and put my arms around her from behind. She was stiff. She stood up slowly. We hugged each other hard.

"We have to notify someone."

She didn't respond.

I took her to my bedroom. I laid her on the bed and put a blanket over her.

"Don't call anyone, please," she said softly.

"No?"

"I'm scared. I'm scared."

I lay down beside her and there we stayed for a long time, kissing and caressing each other as we had never done before. It was as if both of us knew at each moment exactly the kind of caress that the other needed or desired.

■

When I woke up it was already dark. She was asleep. With my gaze fixed on a little crack in the ceiling, I began to think about the future, first the immediate, more or less foreseeable future, which can—or so we think—be controlled; and then the further future, distant and mysterious, which no one can foresee, but only dimly and vaguely intuit. I thought of Señor Blanco, Señor Blanco's corpse, no doubt already stiff with rigor mortis. I understood Severina's fear. But what, I wondered, were we going to do now? If we didn't report the death to a doctor, or the police, or a lawyer, we'd be creating what at that point I saw as unnecessary problems. We had to call an undertaker to come and get the body . . . unless we got rid of it ourselves.

Along with various images of funeral rites, derived from the anthropological reading that, over the years, has formed or deformed my ideas about the end of human life, cruder, sillier, more absurd pictures came to mind, influenced perhaps by sensationalist news reports or macabre films and stories. I saw a pyre made of Severina's books on a mountaintop, against a dawn or dusk sky, and the old man's body twisting and crackling as corpses do when they are purified by fire.

Her eyes were wide open when I turned to her. She pressed her body against mine and asked: "What are we going to do?"

I didn't know what to say.

"I'm afraid," she said again.

"So am I. But we can't let too much time go by."

She nodded emphatically. I got out of bed and began to get dressed. As I put on my shirt, the shadow of my arms, projected by the bedside lamp onto her body and the sheets, reminded me of a bird, and I tried to suppress the thought that it might be a bird of ill omen.

When I was dressed, I sat on the edge of the bed and laid my arm across her; she turned over and looked into my eyes.

"He doesn't have papers, you know, nor do I. What's going to happen now?"

"Papers?"

"Proof of identity."

"You don't have passports?"

She smiled.

"Yes. We have various passports. They're all fake."

"Are you serious?"

She made me move my arm so that she could sit up.

"I never thought all this would happen here, in this country." She looked at the window, and I guessed that she was thinking of some distant place, in Umbria perhaps, where she had said she spent her childhood. "I didn't think he'd die . . . I don't know. I don't know anything."

She covered her face with her hands, and her body began to shake as she broke down, crying quietly but abundantly. I tried to hug her again. She wouldn't let me.

I stood up and left the room. I shut the door behind me and went to sit on the divan, where I had wept for the deaths of my mother and my father. I don't know how many minutes passed before she came out of the bedroom. She was no longer naked and her tears had stopped, but her eyes were bloodshot and the pallor of her face alarmed me. She crossed the living room and dropped down beside me.

"There's something I still haven't told you," she said.

◼

Ahmed had visited her grandfather the day before he had the stroke; that is, the day the old man had come to the bookstore.

"He wanted us to pay him. But we couldn't, of course," said Severina.

Her weary expression, the tone of her voice, the way she half-closed her eyes: all this helped me to guess what was coming, at least in part.

"He proposed that we get married. A Moroccan-style wedding, a Muslim wedding, can you imagine? Me, converting to Islam?"

She forced herself to laugh.

"Did he fall in love with you?"

She shrugged her shoulders.

"Maybe. I don't know."

"Of course he did." I thought: In a way, I've succeeded where Ahmed failed. Luck was on my side.

"He and my grandfather talked in private," Severina continued. "I don't know what they said, but I guess Ahmed threatened him."

I remembered her grandfather's words: "We have been accused of all sorts of crimes . . ."

"Possibly. And maybe Ahmed's visit brought on your grand-father's stroke."

She covered her face with her hands and started crying again.

■

"We have to think about the body, my love, the corpse."

It was the first time I had addressed her in that way, but she didn't seem surprised.

"Yes," she said. "But you still don't understand: we're pariahs. We can't go to an embassy with those passports. They'll realize."

"Do you want me to talk to a lawyer?"

"No, don't, please. I hate lawyers."

"I wonder," I said, thinking aloud, "how bodies get to La Verbena."

"La Verbena?"

"The cemetery where they take the John Does, the unidenti-fied bodies. But . . . don't cry, please. I'm sorry . . ."

She stopped, but only for a moment.

■

When she finished crying she had made up her mind. She wiped her eyes and cheeks with the back of her hand. She swallowed. She tossed her hair back. She looked at me.

"What time is it?" she asked.

It was nine.

"Good," she said. "What say we go for a spin, the three of us?"

"The three of us?"

"Have you got a shovel? We're going to bury him, I don't know where, though. Have you got any ideas?"

I thought for a moment.

"Maybe."

"Where?"

"In a forest, beyond Pinula." I looked out east to the peaks of the mountains that were visible on the far horizon from the windows of my apartment. "It's a really remote spot. No one goes there. They opened up a track a few years ago, but it's never used. I think we could get in there now, because it hasn't rained for a while. When the rain begins, it'll be impassable until the end of the wet season."

"Have you got a shovel?"

"Yes. I've got a shovel."

■

Everyone knows that it's much harder to carry a dead body than a living one; but until you actually do it yourself, you don't realize that the difficulty is as much psychological as physical. What you're shifting is a container that once held life, the conscious life we share, which isn't ours to keep. Nevertheless, conveying the corpse from the apartment to the car wasn't as hard as it might have been. It was late and we were lucky: no one saw us going into the elevator or coming out, or getting into the car. We left the city behind and climbed toward Don Justo, in the mountains. We turned off toward Pinula. We came to a police checkpoint, but they didn't stop us.

"We're in luck."

"So it seems."

"What was that?"

"Gas. Dead bodies go on releasing gas," she said.

We left the village behind, passed Hacienda Nueva and El Cortijo, the golf club and the riding club. We took the dirt road that leads to Mataquescuintla.

"Is this the right way?" she asked when I stopped at a gate.

"Yes."

I got out to open it. Pulling away, I felt the tires skidding on the mud for a few seconds before they got traction, and the car swerved slightly. The rank smell of the mud came in with the breeze.

The track had become even narrower; now it was just two deep ruts with the jungle rising up on either side, dark and somewhat threatening, and the tall weeds scratching shrilly at the underside of the car. Soon we began to climb a steep slope. The climatic conditions changed abruptly. There was a cold wet gust of air and we were enveloped by a mass of thick fog, which the car's headlights could not penetrate.

"Let's stop here, shall we?" she said.

"We're almost there."

After two or three hairpin bends we reached the top of the ridge. The fog cleared. Far off in the distance we could see the lights of a village at the foot of the mountains, and much, much farther away, twinkling among the trees—some of which were slender-trunked and tall, while others were stocky, with twisted, ghostly branches, burdened with creepers—the nebula of the city's lights.

"What a strange place," she said.

Everything seemed to be liquid. A memory from years before suddenly came back to me: a hallucination induced by the psilocybin in mushrooms that grow in that area—a general impression of wateriness, the intuition of a liquid world.

I said: "It's like driving underwater. Look at those trees."

"This is the bottom of the sky!" she exclaimed.

The track started climbing again, heading straight for the highest point on the ridge, which was covered with little trees. We came to a small clearing, where the wheel ruts stopped. I turned the car around and switched off the motor.

"This is it. We'll have to take him a little bit farther. There's a gully."

The air smelled of moss. For a while we watched the trees swaying under a sky so full of stars it was white.

Between the two of us, we carried the old man's body. We went about fifty yards into the trees, slipping repeatedly. We stopped at the edge of a gully plunging away into the shadows, in which a big vein of black rock was dimly visible.

"This is good," she said.

We placed the body carefully between two smooth, wet stones. Without a word, I moved away. She knelt down beside him. She kissed him once on the forehead. Without betraying any sign of pain, she pulled out a handful of her hair and slowly scattered it over his body. She prayed, I think, or maybe recited some lines of poetry. She was like the celebrant of a simple and primitive rite.

I picked up the shovel. I plunged it into the soft, sandy soil. She scooped up a little in both hands. "May it lie softly on you," she murmured as she sprinkled it over her grandfather's chest. She stood up and asked me to finish the burial.

A few steps away, in the starlight, an armadillo waddled slowly past and disappeared into the shadows.

It didn't take me long. I was sweating, and I sensed that there were moments of unhappiness in store for me.

She came over to the mound of earth beneath which her grandfather lay and placed stones in a little pile over his chest, which reminded me of the cairns that people build in rural Morocco, beside paths or in out-of-the-way places, to serve, perhaps, as memorials.

"Someone's going to find him here, sooner or later," she said when we were back in the car.

"I doubt it."

We didn't talk on the trip back to the apartment. I don't know what she was thinking about. I was trying not to think at all.

Nevertheless, I ended up thinking about various things. I was afraid that with the old man gone everything would be different between us. I was afraid she'd distance herself from me. I thought about the possibility of traveling, fleeing. I thought: "I need money."

■

The next few days were calm. On Tuesday, as usual, Severina got up very early and went out to avoid an encounter with Juana. I tried to read a book by Fernando Ortiz, a Cuban disciple of Lombroso, about witchcraft in Cuba, but I couldn't concentrate. A number of times, I went to the windows and looked out to the southeast, where, on the far horizon, I could see the mountaintop where we had buried the enigmatic Señor Blanco.

Juana arrived at the usual time. She went into the kitchen, made some noise, and came into the living room to say hello.

"Did the old gentleman wake up?"

"Yes, thank God."

"And the customer went too?"

"No. Don't call her the customer, OK?"

She nodded and then, with a gesture, requested permission to vacuum the living room. I took refuge in my study.

■

Schnitzler was right, I said to myself: "A woman can leave you for lack of love, or excess of love, for this or that, for everything or nothing." Severina didn't take anything that wasn't hers—not even the key to the apartment, which she left on the little shelf by the door—and this struck me as further proof of ingratitude. Nor did she leave a note, a word of explanation. One Wednesday afternoon when I was at the bookstore, she simply gathered her few belongings, which all fitted into a backpack, left the apartment, and didn't return.

The fact that she didn't have genuine proof of identity, the way her accent shifted, like her grandfather's, the old guy's strange ideas, their peculiar way of life, even her skill at outwitting alarm systems: all of this suggested that our love affair had been a trick, not a trick performed by two human beings in order to deceive a third, but a product of my own delirious imagination. Except that I wasn't crazy. I had proof that both of them had existed: the list of stolen books, Ahmed's testimony (unless he was in on the scheme), and Juana's, and the hospital bills.

I spent the night waiting for the sun to come up so that I could do something. I called Ahmed. He had no news.

"But they haven't left the country, my friend; I put them under a restriction order," he said.

I called the Pensión Carlos. They hadn't seen Severina. I drove around. I must have covered half the city. Predictably, every time I saw a woman, I thought for a moment it was her. I went to the airport, but this time I couldn't go in. I came back home and, deep in the nightmare now, called the Missing Persons' Bureau. A woman's voice answered. She asked for my name and details. I hung up.

I tried to write—to get this crazy story off my chest. I didn't last even fifteen minutes at the desk. When I went back out it was midday. Workers were lined up to buy bread in front of the bakery on the corner. The woman who was serving had long black hair like Severina. I stopped and stood there staring at her for a while. She smiled at me. I walked on. Without realizing what I was doing, I headed for the Pensión Carlos. I stopped for a moment in front of the door. I felt like crying. I walked on aimlessly. I came to the center of the city. My feet were aching. I went into a little cantina, ordered a quart of rum, and sat down to drink. It burned all the way down. I left a bill on the table and walked out. It was starting to get dark. I took a taxi home.

Around seven there was a knock on the door. I put my notebook and pen away in a desk drawer and went to see who it was. It was her!

"What happened? Where were you?" There was dust and grass on her clothes and her backpack.

"Can I come in?"

She left the backpack by the door, and we went and sat on the divan. It was the first time I had been angry with her.

"Where did you go? Look at you! What happened?"

"I went to see my grandfather. I lit a candle on his grave."

"What? Couldn't you have told me? You left your key. I thought you'd gone for good and I'd never see you again."

"I told you, didn't I? Life is shit."

"Can't you explain?"

She was looking at her hands, which were dirty, and glancing up at me from time to time. "I was confused, I am confused. I thought of leaving, yes. I tried. But I couldn't."

"Leaving? To go where?"

"Back to Uruguay; I've got a return ticket. But I couldn't use it. I'm under a restriction order."

Silently, I thanked Ahmed.

"Couldn't you have said?"

"I hate goodbyes."

"So?"

I thought she was going to cry; she tossed her hair back and looked at me steadily.

"I told you. I was confused. I don't like the thought of being completely dependent on you. Can't you understand that?"

"It's not easy."

"Of course not."

We sat there in silence. I turned and looked out the window at a little column of white smoke hanging over the mountains. Maybe I did understand her. Maybe in her place I would have done something similar, I thought. Maybe I was just waiting for her to ask for forgiveness.

"Can't you forgive me?" she asked.

She's made me so happy, I thought, surely I can forgive her for these hours of torment.

"Let's forget it."

She put her arms around my neck.

"Can you promise me something?"

"Maybe."

"Promise that next time you'll say goodbye, at least."

"Let's hope that moment never comes. But look . . ." She showed me the spoils of the day:

Psychic Autobiography
The Seven Who Fled
Voyage to Mount Athos
Viva Mexico!
Reminders of Bouselham

"Did you know you can read it backward?" she said. "In fact, that's how it was written."

We started to read *Reminders* backward, sentence by sentence.

■

"Tell me the story of your life."

"We have many lives," she replied.

Her schooling had not been traditional; Señor Blanco had taken care of it himself, and that was the source of what she called her special sense of freedom.

"Traditionally, children are familiarized with lying from the start. Lying, he used to say, is a necessity. It begins with the myth of Father Christmas, who was originally a figure in Turkish folklore, wasn't he? An unsustainable lie. But by the time it's wearing thin, there are new lies to replace it. Heaven and Hell. Universal Love. Democracy. And then they try to teach them morality, huh!" She paused. "You know, my grandfather used to say that one of our remote ancestors invented dice. A man from Lydia. It's in Herodotus. His people emigrated to the north of Italy because of a famine that lasted for many years."

I hadn't realized it until then, but for me Severina had become a pure object of pleasure. Like books. I wondered what I meant to her. "You're more interested in books than in me, aren't you?" I said, and regretted it immediately.

She looked at me without a word. A little later on, she asked: "Do you remember the first time we talked? I mean, when you shut me in. You were lying about the cameras, weren't you? I lied about my cell phone too!"

"How do you deactivate the alarms?"

"That's a secret."

"Will you tell me one day?"

"Maybe. But then it wouldn't be a secret, and that would be a pity."

We laughed.

"We should always be together," she said.

"Really? Forever?"

"Forever."

I was thinking it would be impossible. I smiled. "All right. Forever."

We hugged. We went on talking. Until the telephone rang. It was Ahmed. He wanted to know if she was there.

"Yes, she's here."

"You got her, eh, partner?" He laughed. "I'll be there in half an hour. If you don't mind, of course."

"We'll be expecting you."

Severina sat back on the divan, pulled up her legs, and put her arms around her knees. She looked worried. "Ahmed? You told him to come?"

"He wants to get a few things straight. So that's what we're going to do."

"Couldn't it wait?"

"I don't think so."

She wasn't happy. "All right. Whatever you like," she said.

"Trust me."

"I trust you. Of course I trust you. But I don't understand. What's with this Moroccan guy?"

"He's going to help us."

"To do what?"

"To get out of here. To start again somewhere else."

"I don't want to start anything anywhere."

"Don't you?"

"I want to keep traveling from place to place; I want to go on doing what I've always done up till now."

"With me?"

"Yes."

"Then we need to get out of here. At least until we're sure that no one's going to investigate the disappearance of your grandfather."

"You're right about that," she said.

I lay down beside her. She stretched out her legs so I could rest my head on her thighs. And we stayed like that, hardly moving—she ran her fingers through my hair—and talked while we waited for Ahmed.

When the call came from reception to say that our visitor had arrived, she got up, went into the bedroom, and shut the door.

■

Ahmed came in with a broad smile on his face.

"Nice place," he said, surveying the living room, the dining room, the view of buildings and mountains from the windows. "Good for you. And the little vixen?"

"Tea? Mint? Black?"

"Mint. And the old guy?"

"I wanted to talk to you about that."

"Is he here?"

I shook my head.

"Where is he?"

"Why did you tell me they were married?"

Ahmed laughed. "A joke, my friend."

Severina came out of the bedroom. She crossed the living room and greeted Ahmed with a kiss on each cheek, French style.

"You're more beautiful than ever," said Ahmed.

"You too." She looked him up and down.

We made tea and went to sit at the low table in the sitting room.

"We're planning to travel. You said you'd taken out a restriction order."

"I had no choice. I want them to pay me what they owe; that's the way it is."

"OK. I think we can pay you. In kind."

Ahmed raised his eyebrows. There was an awkward silence.

"With books." I swept my arm around, pointing at the walls of the living room, covered with books.

"Why not?" replied Ahmed.

"And you'll remove the restriction order?"

"I'll be happy to, once we settle. But what about the old guy? Where is he?"

Severina didn't attempt to lie. She explained.

∎

We did a series of calculations. Then I invited Ahmed to look through my bookshelves and take what he liked as payment for the debt.

In a few minutes, he chose about a hundred books. Then he paused. "This still isn't enough," he said.

Severina looked at me; she was indignant. "How is that possible?" she asked.

Ahmed went on picking out books and piling them on the table.

I offered him more tea and went to the kitchen to make it. Severina followed me.

"He's picked out about two hundred books there," she said in a whisper. "Are you going to let him take them all?"

"I'll let him take as many as he likes, as long as he leaves us in peace."

"*I could kill him!*" she hissed, with a surprising vehemence. Then she walked out of the kitchen, went straight to the bedroom, and slammed the door behind her.

■

In the living room, Ahmed had made eight piles of books of varying heights. "That'll do it," he said.

I served him a second cup of tea and we sat down again, facing each other. He had his back to the bedroom door.

"What's up with Ana?" he asked.

"I don't think she could bear to watch the plundering."

Ahmed laughed and looked over his shoulder. "Strange people," he said quietly, after a moment. "You never know what they're going to do. I don't trust them. But you've been lucky, it seems."

Severina appeared behind him. She was holding a book: hardback, octavo, not very thick. She looked at the table and the piles of books.

"Ahmed," she said, and he gave a little start, "you're so greedy."

"Greedy?" He turned to look at her.

"I didn't take half that many from your store, and they weren't all as good."

Ahmed noticed the book she was holding. "What have you got there?"

"I'm going to offer you this book," she said, "in exchange for all those ones." She pointed to the piles on the table.

Ahmed looked at her, then at the piles, then back at her. "Can I have a look?"

Severina handed it over.

"What . . . ," he asked, "what is this book?" He was leafing through it with his mouth slightly open. I came and looked over his shoulder, eagerly reading what I could here and there. On some of the pages there were handwritten notes in the margins. It was the mother of all books, the holy Koran.

I looked at Severina, who looked back with an invisible smile.

■

"I lied to you," she said softly, but not so softly that Ahmed couldn't hear as well. "I took this book, just this one, from Borges's library. The notes are his. There, in the margin, he started writing one of his stories."

" 'The Mirror of . . . '? Is this possible?" said Ahmed, without taking his eyes off the book. "Are you trying to trick me?"

"You decide," Severina said calmly.

■

In the end, Ahmed took the Koran and relinquished my books. After amicable discussions with my partners, I sold my share in La Entretenida at a profit. Appealing to reasons that I never fully understood, Severina convinced me that a false passport was well worth having. She prepared one for me with the skill of a professional counterfeiter. That was how I acquired the name Blanco; Severina and I became relatives. (The idea of belonging to a line of people who lived exclusively for and by books delighted me and flattered my vanity.) Shortly afterward, we took a flight to Mexico City. It was only when the plane had taken off, and the Valle de la Virgen and the volcanoes were disappearing into the distance among the patchy June clouds that she said: "See. It's all different now." She gave me a kiss on the ear, and I shivered. "The notes were forged, you know, though almost identical to the ones in the original."

Ahmed, who regarded himself as an expert on the works and handwriting of Borges, had accepted the book because he was confident that sooner or later he'd find a buyer: a learned fool or a swindler, in either case, a snob. Maybe he would sell it for a fortune one day. Maybe not.

And maybe one day Severina will tear out some of her hair and scatter it over my body.

ACKNOWLEDGMENTS

The aphorisms of Yoshida Kenko on page 14 are from *Essays in Idleness: The Tsurezuregusa of Kenko,* translated by Donald Keene (New York: Columbia University Press, 1998). The quotation from Rubén Darío's "Canto de esperanza" ("Song of Hope") on page 21 is from *Stories and Poems/Cuentos y poesías,* translated by Stanley Appelbaum (Mineola, New York: Dover Publications, 2002).

RODRIGO REY ROSA is perhaps the most prominent writer on the Guatemalan literary scene. Along with the work of writers like Roberto Bolaño, Horacio Castellanos Moya, and Fernando Vallejo, Rey Rosa's fiction has been widely translated and internationally acclaimed. His books include *Dust on Her Tongue*, *The Beggar's Knife*, and *The Pelcari Project*, all of which were translated into English by the late Paul Bowles. In addition to his many novels and story collections, Rey Rosa has translated books by Bowles, Norman Lewis, François Augiéras, and Paul Léautaud.

CHRIS ANDREWS was born in Newcastle, Australia, in 1962. He teaches at the University of Western Sydney. Among other works of fiction by Latin American authors, he has translated Roberto Bolaño's *By Night in Chile* (New Directions, 2003) and César Aira's *Shantytown* (New Directions, 2013). His book of poems *Lime Green Chair* (Waywiser, 2012) won the 2011 Anthony Hecht Poetry Prize.